MAKE MINE VENGEANCE

Other books by Robert Colby

Fiction

MAKE MINE VENGEANCE

ROBERT COLBY

WILDSIDE PRESS
Berkeley Heights, New Jersey

First Wildside Press edition: January 2001

Make Mine Vengeance
A publication of
Wildside Press
P.O. Box 45
Gillette, NJ 07933-0045
www.wildsidepress.com

SECOND EDITION

Chapter One

His name was Gil Ballard. And though at 31 he was six feet two inches tall and weighed 203 pounds, much of it muscle, he was easygoing and had not been mad enough to bruise anyone for years.

Until now.

Until this moment at two o'clock in the morning where across the road from where his car was parked, a bar called the Gold Reef was locking its doors and blacking its lights.

Of course he had been angry enough to kill three men twenty-three days and five hours ago. But that had been quite impossible because at the time he had been conscious only for short periods. And though in two days he recovered his wits, it was three weeks before he got out of the hospital. Three weeks while they returned what had been a very straight and well-proportioned nose to a reasonable facsimile of the same; while they patched a wide good-humored mouth so that it could smile again — if it wanted to — and not reveal anything of the ugly, three-tooth gap that had been bridged with good dentistry. They also had to mend the clean shelf of jaw, sew the cuts under the quietly intelligent gray-green eyes and reduce the right temple swelling below the dark wave of hair.

Altogether it had been a neat job all seven hundred and fifty dollars worth. And while the face had never been pretty, it was still handsome in a rugged way and the scars didn't show except on very close inspection. But there were scars that were not of the face.

But perhaps the hardest part to take was that the beating had been so completely unnecessary. It was about as motivated as some of those teenage-gang clubbings of strangers. And these men had passed adolescence long ago.

Motivated or not, someone was going to pay. And only part of the payment would be financial.

The Gold Reef was dark now. Everyone had left but the bartender-owner Beef Costigan. He was a ponderous, balding ape of a man with the squat chunkiness of a wrestler. No one seemed to know anything about him except that he had come south from Chicago with enough coin to set up the Gold Reef on coast Highway A1A above Miami and south of the swank area known as Golden Beach.

Ballard got out of his Pontiac and walked across the road to the darkened parking area beside the bar. A pale blue Olds was the single remaining car in the lot. It figured to belong to Costigan, so Ballard leaned against a fender and waited.

He saw now that there was a faint illumination from a window near the side door which he had not been able to glimpse from the road. When this too winked off, he flipped the cigarette he had been smoking into darkness and watched the door attentively.

In a moment Costigan came out, fumbled with the lock and lumbered over to the Olds. He did not see

Ballard until he was almost on top of him.

"What the hell!" he said, and paused in midstride to peer into the gloom. "Who's that?"

"Come here and see, Costigan."

"That you, Marty?"

Ballard did not reply and Costigan moved in closer with a wary step. When he paused again three feet away, Ballard took the pencil flash from his pocket and shined it on his own face.

Costigan craned forward, said, "Who the goddamn hell are you?"

"What do you think, Costigan? Did they do a good job gluing the pieces back together?"

"Christ!" said Costigan. "Ballard, ain't it?"

"That's right, Costigan. They let me out of the hospital this morning. Three weeks and two days, seven hundred and fifty bucks worth of patching and stitching, toss in free phony teeth." He lowered the light.

"So? What ya want with me? I didn't have nothin' to do with it."

"You stood there and watched it happen, Costigan. I didn't see you interfere."

"Hell," said Costigan, "guys like that it don't pay to interfere."

"What do you mean, guys like that? Sounds like you know them, Costigan."

"Nah. I don't know 'em. They ain't been in maybe . . . two, three times."

"Sure, that's what you told the police. But while I was sitting at the bar, you were in a real chummy huddle with them over in a corner."

"Just passin' the time."

"Costigan — listen to me. You're gonna pass some time on your back if I don't get those names. A whole lot of time. You're a lousy liar."

"Don't get hard with me, pal. I tole the cops, I tell you, I don't know those bums."

Ballard could see that Costigan was not the type to be convinced with conversation. He pocketed the flash and moved in. He gave the barkeep two sharp open-handed blows across the face and followed it with a piston jab to the belly that made Costigan do a groaning bend.

He didn't see the knife until Costigan had sneaked it out of his back pocket and flicked the long blade open.

"I'm gonna cut you," said Beef Costigan. "I'm gonna eat you good. This time you won't be back."

Until now the anger in Ballard had been idling, waiting to thrust itself at the real enemy. But the knife brought a change in him. As with the episode in the bar, there again was a sneaky advantage. The knife multiplied the forces against him unfairly so that the bartender seemed to join the opposition openly when he flashed the blade.

Ordinarily Ballard would have had a justifiable fear of the knife. But now it only triggered the hatred that had been building in him.

"That was where you made your big mistake, Beef," he said pleasantly. "You would have been all right if you'd just answered a few questions and kept that toy in your pocket."

Costigan advanced with the blade held low. His movements were uncertain, cautious. Apparently he did not understand men who were not afraid of a knife.

Ballard stood immobile and waited. But when the knife arced upward at him, he side-stepped gracefully and hammered Costigan's ear with a blow that staggered him off balance. The second blow fell on the side of Costigan's jaw before he could recover. Ballard caught him from behind as he was falling and hammer-locked his windpipe until the knife hand was limp and he was able to reach out and pluck it from loose fingers. Then he pulled Costigan to the ground and swung over him, pinning his arms with the heavy grind of knees.

Now Ballard touched the point of the knife to the tender spot just below Costigan's right eye. "I won't make you guess what I'm going to do next," he said. "I'm going to perform a little surgery, Costigan. I want your face to look like mine did. Let's see — first we'll slice around the eyes, then the head and the nose. From there we'll slash the lips a bit. And while we're at it, we'll bash in a few teeth and finish by carving the jaw."

He meant to do none of these things but Beef Costigan was a primitive type who would be persuaded only with the primitive elements of fear and self-preservation.

"Don't!" said Costigan, sobbing for breath. "Please! I didn't have nothin' to do with it."

Ballard made the knife point sink a fraction deeper in the socket under the eye. "I might change my mind and kill you," he said. "Give me the names of those men. Come on. Quick!"

"I'm scared," he said. "They'd murder me."

"You want to die now or later? Come on. Hurry it up!"

Costigan moistened his lips. "I don't know their last names. Just one of them — Gould, Russ Gould."

"Gould," snorted Ballard. "Where did you dig that one up?"

"That's the name he goes by. I swear it! Russ Gould."

"Which one was he?"

"One with the black hair, good-lookin'. The young one."

"The one with the smile and the pretty teeth?"

"Yeah."

"Where does he live?"

"He . . . I don't know."

"Sure you do, you lying bastard. Guess I'll have to slice you."

"No! He lives up the coast a couple of miles on A1A. Golden Beach."

"What number?"

"Eleven-thirty-nine. You won't tell him, will ya?"

Ballard didn't answer but began to run his hands over Costigan's pockets. A suspicious bulge proved to be a .32 snub-nosed revolver. "Why didn't you use this?" he said.

"Didn't wanna kill you, just scare you."

Ballard folded the blade into the sheath, put gun and knife in his pocket, stood up. "You go near a phone," he said, "you tip Gould I'm coming and I'll be back to finish you."

"I'm a clam," he said. "I swear it. If I tole him where you got the word, he'd butcher me."

"And if he didn't, I would," said Ballard. "Remember that. Now you lie right there until I'm out of sight. Then you beat it for your rathole while you're still lucky."

He walked away without looking back, got in his car and drove off in the direction of Golden Beach.

Chapter Two

As Ballard rode along the highway he thought what a strange thing it was that this could happen to a pretty ordinary citizen. At least one who was ordinary in the sense that he had never committed a crime or played on the fringe with criminals, never been in jail, never got into a jam worse than a ticket for speeding. And while he had made his life interesting and sometimes exciting, they were usually not interests or excitements that would bring him trouble.

True, he was not a stranger to the ways of crime and criminals, for many a summer night between terms at Michigan State had found him in the back seat of a homicide prowl ear behind Detective Walt Lundberg, whose son Clay played end with Ballard on the sane team.

Clay was not the least interested in his father's profession. He was crazy about planes and wanted to be a commercial pilot. But Ballard had the passing notion that some day he would like to become a detective and begged Clay's dad fort some firsthand knowledge. Walt Lundberg agreed a little reluctantly, as passengers were not exactly regulation and he had to go to some trouble to arrange it with the brass, getting even the cooperation of his own patrol duty partner.

Once having undertaken this education in crime detection, Ballard went at it with the same determination with which he tackled anything that interested him. Not only did he learn all about weapons, lab science, radio codes, hoodlum MOs and the legal process, but he also discovered the practical applications of force skillfully, if not always dangerously, applied. The homicide crew did not deal only with killings, but with anything in the nature of violence. And once or twice during some barroom mêlée, Lundberg and his partner had the surprise — if not the official pleasure — of finding Ballard right in there slugging, making it a trio.

But when Ballard found that glamorous detective work was a rarity, that it was mostly routine and often pretty dull, that the general run of culprits was slightly above the moron level and that the pay scale was at best discouraging, he lost interest.

Presently he was the owner of a cracker-box radio station in Fort Lauderdale. But though it was small, it was busy, so busy that six months ago he had been offered three times the thirty-six thousand dollars it had cost him to set it up in a field on the outskirts of town a few years back.

Me had lived in Detroit and he had gone to Michigan State where his size, his native skill and endless practice made him an outstanding fullback. He came out of his four years with All-American and still had good grades. For a time he played pro, until a leg fracture closed one door and opened another.

When he got back to Detroit has reputation had preceded him and he was offered a spot with one of the big-chain radio-TV outlets as sportscaster. He had a decent voice, he knew sports and the sports world knew him. After a few years of mastering his technique, he built himself a good following and picked up sponsors. And from sponsors came larger and larger fees and a sweet chunk of money to add to his savings from pro ball.

Eventually he became head of the sports department and then program manager for the radio division.

On a winter vacation to Florida, he fell in love with Fort Lauderdale, the atmosphere, the climate. He decided that another radio station in the town could shoulder itself into competition. His father agreed to lend him the additional money he needed if he could get the FCC to grant him a license.

The license was approved and in three years he had repaid his father and had a going business.

Of women there had been many. He had loved them casually and left them easily for one reason or another until, his sportscasting days, he met Julie Harmon. She was a singer on the station and sometimes she appeared in those one-minute "live" commercials. She was a willowy woman with a trim figure, a sweet-soft face and a voice to match.

He got lost over her and there was an engagement and there were plans for a wedding in six months. But it never happened.

There are no holidays in the radio-TV business. So on New Year's Eve preceding the projected spring marriage, there were programs to prepare and broadcast. There was a party that he and Julie were to attend and she asked if she might go on ahead of him. He said he would join her there just before midnight.

But before midnight, she was dead.

She had been traveling across town to the party with another couple. They had had no more than two drinks apiece and were moving at a normal dip when a speeding drunk slashed through an intersection against a red light and hit them broadside. The other two were seriously injured, the drunk was unscathed, and of course it was Julie who was killed.

He never really got over it. On the surface the wound healed, but underneath there was a throbbing ache that wouldn't stop. Meanwhile he busied himself with any number women, never gaining lasting satisfaction and never gaining lasting satisfaction and never marrying.

He supposed that, however indirectly, it was the return of that ache that caused his trouble a little over three weeks ago. . . .

He had gone to a cocktail party at the Americana Hotel in Miami Beach. It was given by one of the big record companies to promote the spinning of their platters on local stations. The party was primarily for disc jockeys and station executives, since from these the best results could be wheedled. Ballard had a date, which fell through at tine last minute, and decided to go alone.

There was the usual confusion of milling people, most of whom were unknown to each other, slopping free drinks and going half boozed to a roast beef dinner liberally sprinkled with moist speeches and corny jokes. Bored, Gil Ballard stayed for only a small part of the dance that followed. He left around ten.

He was still feeling his drinks and he had no idea why he chose to stop at the Gold Reef except that the need for a nightcap struck hurt a moment before he came abreast of it. He had never been there before.

It was a small place with a gaudy façade and a bright sprinkling of neon. Inside, there was a row of booths in a long, narrow room, a bar opposite. Against the far wall between the Ladies and Gents signs there was a giant red jukebox with the usual lights, push buttons and song cards. This was blaring loudly in the darkened room.

The place was practically deserted. Three men sat at the end of the bar in conversation with the chunky bartender, who nodded as he leaned toward them wiping a glass. Two couples made up the remainder of the customers and, shortly after Ballard took a seat at the bar, they left their booth, paid up and went out.

So engrossed was the chunky bartender in his conversation with the three men that even after Ballard got his attention, he seemed reluctant to take the order, filling it with a hasty nothing and returning immediately to the bar.

Ballard was in a foul mood. It was one of those times when the wound opened and Julie stole into his consciousness unaware. He remembered little snatches of conversation, the look of her as she stood before the cameras adjusting her smile in the seconds before the opening of her show, the whisper-softness of her touch as she caressed him in the darkness of a parked car.

Suddenly the record in the jukebox came to a bleating dose and the silence which followed was a much more devastating impingement on his thoughts.

He gave the machine a glance, then ambled over and began rotating the card index for a song he liked. He knew a moment of happy-sad elation when he came across Julie's old theme song, the one she used for her show. He put a coin in the slot, pressed the appropriate button and returned to his seat. Listening to the soft strains, he ordered another drink from the disgruntled bartender and allowed himself to sink into a rather maudlin nostalgia.

Still unsatisfied at the song's conclusion, he played it again and then a third time, telling himself it would certainly be the last.

But as the song began anew, one of the three men broke away and shuffled over with a toothpick in his mouth. He was slightly above average height, had wide shoulders, wore a tan suit with a chalk stripe. He was swarthy, had a narrow face with a long, sharp nose. His eyes had a droopy look that was at once smug and sleepy. He wore a diamond-studded tie clasp.

"Hey, bud," he said, the toothpick bobbing, "you own that song or somethin'?"

Ballard's eyes roamed over the man and he didn't like his looks any better than his attitude. "I might," he said. "I might own it."

"You play it once more and you will own it," bobbed the toothpick. "You'll get it rapped over your head. So knock it off! Understand?"

"No," said Ballard, feeling the sharp edge of irritation rising above the soggy thing inside him, "I don't understand at all." He turned back to his drink. The hell with him! He wasn't going to play the song again anyway, but he certainly wasn't going to admit it now.

The hand grabbed his arm and turned him around none too gently. The nose, like an aimed stiletto, came closer and there was the strong stink of whisky fumes. "Listen, wise guy, don't give me any crap. I better not hear that tune again."

"And I'll tell *you* something for your own good," said Ballard mildly. "If you don't want your lip cut on your own nose, you'd better toddle back to your friends and keep your mouth shut." Again he turned to his drink.

The man's body moved at his side and once more the face intruded close to has. "Just remember, smart boy — I only ask once." Then the man shuffled back and climbed on his stool.

At any other time, in better spirits, Ballard might have ignored it. He was gentle by nature and there had never been any need to prove his masculinity. He had seldom met anyone he couldn't clobber senseless and for that very reason he was more apt to contain himself. He had an easygoing nature, but this made him the most dangerous of capable fighters, for when finally aroused, his fury was boundless.

In any case, but for his peculiar mood, he might have let this one pass. Yet the anger in him was more than a small thing of the moment. There was a quietly restive interior force that wanted to strike out at the nameless evil which had stolen what he loved most. And at this moment the force was walking in him with a heavy tread.

So he got up and put another coin in the box and played the song yet a fourth time. The sharp-nosed character had his back turned, but his head was slightly cocked in a listening attitude. The bartender and the others were not talking and the silence was electric.

Ballad was climbing on his stool when Julie's theme song spread over tine room. He drank and he listened, paying no attention to the others. It was not an open challenge, just a thin satisfaction which he had already forgotten in the plaintive cry of the song.

He did not see them approach. He felt their presence behind him and he turned.

Sharp Nose merely stared with his sleepy eyes. For the first time Ballard noticed the other two. The big one was about six-four and built like a Sherman tank. He had coarse though not ugly features, but his eyes were a washed-out green and fish-dead.

The third was of average height and downright handsome. He had jet hair, sharp brown eyes, the clearest olive skin. And, though his face was a bit too full, his features were almost perfect. He had a marvelous set of teeth for smiling — which he was broadly doing right then. Smiling on, he spoke. "Thought you were told not to play that song again, friend," he said.

"I have a very good habit of not listening to every grease-ball who tells me what to do," said Ballard. "Now, beat it!"

The smiling one's arm came up and down swiftly. Something diamond-hard struck his temple. It was like the stab of an icicle into his brain. The smile faded — not on the man's face, but from Ballard's consciousness. And when it returned weakly, the big one was holding his arms from behind the bar and the other two were beating his face open in turns, hammering it with the precision of men swinging sledge hammers on a thin spike of resisting steel.

But his face was not so resistant and in the glimmer of consciousness he felt the bridge of his nose let go, the jaw unhinge and the teeth crash inward to float in the drool around his lower gums. And the beating went on and on.

He tried to keep the void from closing in so that he could remember forever the lips parted and the white smile in the olive face. But it faded again and vas lost. And then was replaced by the unsmiling face of the young intern as the ambulance screamed and flew into the night.

The plain-clothes detectives were there at his bed two days later, when the brain concussion gave up and let him live and return to consecutive awareness. And he told them the story and they nodded and shook their heads and took notes and went away and came back and said there was nothing they could do. The bartender admitted that he had had a brief conversation with the men — about baseball. But he did not know them by name anal had seen them only once or twice before as customers. Then, when the fight had started, he was afraid. They were too many for him. A patron arriving just too late called the police. But when the police came, the men were beyond tracing.

The detectives said they would keep working on it. But with so little to go by, the bartender having "dumbly" washed their glasses of prints, there was little hope.

And so Ballard, normally gentle, easygoing, was aroused. He would handle it himself. He had begun. He had a name. It was the right name — a smiling name. And he had an address. And someone was going to pay. And there was going to be more brutality.

But this time all of it was going to belong to him.

Chapter Three

*T*he homes along Golden Beach on the Gold Coast of Florida speak softly, but with unmistakable clarity, of money. Not the kind of money which most people come by in a lifetime of saving in fairly responsible jobs, either. But rather the immense quantities of money which come from the ownership of large enterprises: oil wells pumping liquid gold around the clock, department stores ringing up sales in a hundred or more departments, well-known and little-known inventions paying their endless royalties, chains of restaurants serving, millions, fleets of trucks, hauling, hauling.

Almost all of the houses are large. Some are mansions. Most sit well back from the road on private acres of palm-shaded privacy. All look out upon sandy beaches to the subtropic pulsing of the Atlantic Ocean.

Eleven-thirty-nine was printed on the roadside, rural-type mailbox. And over it — RUSSEL S. GOULD.

The house itself, a low splash of rambling redwood

and stucco in two stories, was in the middle ground between Golden Beach — expensive and mansion — rich. It displayed itself briefly through the driveway openings in the tall growth of ixora hedge.

Strangely, for it was going on 3 a.m., lights glowed from some room in the lower reaches of the house.

Ballard parked his Pontiac convertible on the road side of the hedge. Then he walked silently over the curving drive and sneaked around to the back of the house, noting first that there was a new Chevy parked at the door.

He stood now on a down-sweeping expanse of lawn dotted with royal and coconut palms, orange trees, assorted flowers and vegetation. Below the lawn there was a wide swath of beach losing itself in the restless surge of ocean. One curving end of a swimming pool could be seen jutting from the other side of the house.

The lower back side of the house was one great expanse of glass through which splashed lights from an enormous living room. A sliding glass door leading to a spacious oval of flagstone patio was partially open. From it came the modulated throb of dance music having the bell clarity and tonal refinement of costly hi-fi equipment.

Ballard moved to the shadows and looked in.

There were two young couples in the living room. He could see neither distinctly but it was obvious that both of the women were uncommonly attractive, if not beautiful. Both had startling figures, especially the dark-haired girl dancing with a young man nearly a head shorter in the center of the room.

He could not see the blonde as well, nor her partner. But they sat on a curve of section sofa in a dim corner, unfastening hungry mouths just long enough to swill from tall, narrow glasses.

There was no sign of Russ Gould or his unplayful playmates.

The scene was confusingly average to Ballard and not lowing what else to do, he waited.

In less than ten minutes, the music came to a halt and three minutes later the Chevy had departed with all but the tall girl with the dark hair and abundance of figure. She came back into the living room, stretched and walked toward the patio. She had not taken a down steps before Ballard was around front jamming a finger on the door bell.

She came to the door with a wide-eyed expression of surprise. Her hair dropped with ebony sleekness to her shoulders. Her eyes were large, bright emeralds in a face that just missed static symmetry of feature with a mouth too broad and full and a not unpleasant hint of flashiness in the pout of checks and flare of nose — enough to give the face character and keep it from the dull vacuity of doll-like perfection.

Her legs were extremely long and beautifully tapered. Her waist was slender. She wore a pure-white strapless gown with a painted flush of two red roses at the bodice. Her breasts fell like breaking white waves from the rim of her dress to rise again in straining conical peaks.

"Well," she said quite amiably and with a smile, "who are you?"

"I'm looking for Russ," he parried. "Is he around?"

The casual toss of the name, even at 3:00 in the morning, seemed to increase her friendliness and bring a subtle shade of awe to her tone and manner.

"I'm awfully sorry," she said. "He's not here. I'm afraid you missed him, by a day. He flew to Chicago yesterday."

Ballard studied her, estimated her age at somewhere in the middle twenties.

"Would you like to come in a minute?" she said with the deference one pays to someone of real importance — in this case any friend of Russell Gould's.

"All right," he said. "Why not?" She might have an answer or two. She certainly had everything else. He stepped in and she closed the door.

He followed her to the living room over white rugs of deep pile and, as they went, she said over her shoulder, "You're out pretty late, aren't you?"

"In that, I'm not alone," he said.

"I'm only up, not out," she said. "Besides, I work until two."

They fell into opposite chairs. He looked around. Big stone fireplace — naturally. Heavy modern pieces. The entire room done in black, white, and gold, with touches of red. Rich. In good taste. Marine paintings on the walls, tropic landscapes, wild, impressive. Great arch of sailfish over the mantel. Polished driftwood tables, cloisonné lamps, jade figurines. Money. All money.

"What do you do that keeps you up until two?" he said. "I'm a hostess," she answered, "at the Tropic Owl out near Pompano. You knew Russ owned it, didn't you?"

"Oh, sure," he said. "Sure. He didn't tell me about you, though. Guess he was too busy last tine we met."

"Well, I'm new. I haven't been there a month yet. I suppose you're wondering why I'm here in this house." She said it apologetically, as though she were more an intruder than he was.

"Frankly I *was* wondering, yes."

"I have a little apartment in Lauderdale-by-the-Sea. But Russ said as long as he was going to be gone a while, I should use the house as my own, servants and all. Isn't he wonderful!"

"Fine!" he said. "A really great guy. Does all right by his friends. How long do you think he'll be gone?"

"I can't say. A week or a month. He's so busy. He has so many things going for him — a night club and a boat yard here and I don't know what all around the country."

"Smart," he said, tapping his brow. "A quick mind."

She looked at him with a small measure of uncertainty. He must remember to play it straight. "Where is Russ staying in Chicago? Know where I can reach him?"

She shook her head. "I don't think he knows himself. He's always on the move."

"Doesn't he phone you?"

"Rarely when he's out of town. He's too busy."

"I wouldn't think he'd ever be too busy for you, Miss — or is it Mrs.?"

She smiled. "Neither. Just Paula. Paula Schaeffer. And yours?"

He hesitated. The hell with it. Guy probably never bothered to find out his name — dust a passing incident. "Gil is mine. Gil Ballard."

"Have you worked with Russ on any of his enterprises, Gil?"

"One. Just one. But we were very close at the time. Actually I run a radio station." If she could only sing, he thought. And make it the right song.

"Do you advertise for Russ?"

"Not now. But someday soon." He kept a very straight face.

"Well," she said, "I'm a bad hostess. Not at the Tropic Owl — but to Russ's friends. Wouldn't you like a drink?"

"I would. Bourbon-on-the-rocks."

Long legs unfolded, stood, and moved that supple body with its heady sway of breasts across the room to an alcove bar. Watching her, he was suddenly full of desire. And forgetful of hate.

She brought his bourbon and a rum drink for herself, resumed her seat with another teasing cross of legs.

"Were you having a little party?" he said casually. "I almost scraped fenders with some people on their way out."

"A maroon Chevy?"

"Yes."

"Just some people who work at the club. They're part of the floor show and they sometimes bring me home. Russ said I could use Carl, the chauffeur, but there's no point in keeping him up so late."

He nodded. "Russ didn't tell me he had a boat yard. Big operation?"

"Not large for Miami, maybe. But the second largest in Fort Lauderdale. It's called East Coast Marine. Like most of his businesses, Russ runs it by remote control and pays more attention to his interests in Chicago."

"Oh? Which one of his Chicago enterprises is engaging his talents at the moment?"

She frowned. "You probably know more about him that I do. I never ask questions and I know only what he tells me. He did say something about wholesale liquor distribution with headquarters in Chicago. So I suppose that's it."

"You think highly of Russ, don't you?" he said. And wondered how highly — and how intimately. Gould would have a way with women — and it would be his way.

She smiled but her eyes were careful. "For the time I've known him — about a month — I think a great deal of him. He's very generous. You know, most of the clubs and hotels around here pay you fifty-percent cash and the rest in sunshine. It's considered such a privilege to work here at all that you're lucky if they offer you a living wage. Compared to New York, for instance, the scale is ridiculous. And you can't eat sunshine. Russ pays me about three times what I could get anywhere else. So naturally, I'm not exactly mad at him. Besides he's . . . well, he's quite a guy."

"And very good looking, wouldn't you say?"

She studied him for some special meaning. Beat he kept his face bland. "Oh, yes," she said, "very nice looking. He has a kind of Latin magnetism. And did you ever see such beautiful teeth in your life?"

"No," he said, "never. As a matter of fact, when I get a mental image of Russ, all I can see are those teeth. They fascinate me."

"And that smile," she said. "Charming!"

"Charming."

There was a silence.

"Are you a native of this area?" he asked.

"No. I came down from New York in November, just about six weeks ago. Decided I couldn't stand another northern winter. I did more or less the same kind of work in a New York hotel. I arranged parties and banquets, things like that."

"You came down alone?"

"With a girl friend. But she was just on vacation and couldn't find a decent job so she went back. I was lucky. I answered an ad in the paper and it turned out to be Russ and he hired me — over about twenty others."

"I cam see why."

"No you can't," she said. "I'm very efficient. But thanks — I think."

For Russell Gould a woman would have to be efficient is many ways, he thought, and took his drink across

the room to a rich-looking hi-fi console. He lifted the lid
and went through an assortment of records. He wasn't
too surprised when he found Julie's theme song. It was
a popular song from a vintage year of quality ballads, a
lasting favorite. Smiling, he held up the platter for her
to see.

"This is one Russ would like," he said. "I'll play it
for him. Mind?"

She shook her head and he dropped it on the spindle
with a couple of others, turning on the machine, setting
the controls. Softly, the ballad filled the room.

"Dance?" he said.

"It's terribly late."

"Yes, isn't it?"

She shrugged, got up and came to him. They
danced.

She was a lot of woman but she maneuvered like
power steering. The press of her against him was about
as calming as holding a cushioned rocket in your arms
at blast-off.

"A song like this one can get you into a lot of
trouble," he said.

"Oh? Tell me about it," she murmured into his ear.

"Some of it is hard trouble," he said: "And some soft
— like now."

She laughed. "You're not making a bit of sense."

"Does anything?"

"You sound bitter." She looked up at him with a
moist parting of those full, sensual lips, her expression
amused, quizzical. The music sobbed and somehow got
mixed up with the perfume scent of her hair. And what
the song had meant and what it had done to him was
forgotten.

"You're much too nice to be bitter," she was saying.
There was hypnotic suggestion in the cadence of her

words, the very tilt of her head.

"Bitterness is a bad taste in my mouth," he said in a faraway voice. "I wonder if you could take it away?"

And then he kissed her and they weren't dancing but the cushioned rocket was flipping over and taking a long power dive. The power was in the cling of her body and the thrust was her tongue searching.

"Does that help?" she murmured when they undid themselves.

"It helps. But there's a lot of bitterness to overcome."

He kissed her again and led her to the patio where they fell upon the cushions of a rattan sofa. The record changed and there was the sound of a tune without bitterness.

They talked not at all. He did not give her time for conversation. Her breasts heaved, his hand wandered over them and she didn't complain. Not when he loosened the zipper either, and brought her half naked against him. Not when he kissed the tips of those marvelous conical peaks. But rather when his hand got too lost beneath the fold of her skirt and the lace trim of filmy undergarments.

Then she said in a hoarse whisper, "There's a point of no, return, Gil. And before we reach it, I'd like to turn bark. Okay?"

"Do I have a choice?"

"No. I'm afraid not. But it was a beautiful trip — as far as it went . . ."

Not two minutes later they were walking to the door and she was saying, "You'll have to come out to the Tropic Owl and see the show. And also, me."

He was about to agree but it took him a moment to sap so. His glance had climbed a short flight of stairs to a railed hallway. A man was leaning on the rail, looking down. He was a tall, wiry-looking man, tense, tolled. He was young. He had sandy hair and carved features.

He wore dark trousers and an Eisenhower jacket. His hair was rumpled, as if he had come recently from sleep. He held his position, motionless. His eyes were unblinking and he watched with the bold arrogance of possession.

The sight of him was lost as they came to the door.

"You weren't even listening," she said.

"Yes, I was. The Tropic Owl. When?"

"Why not tomorrow night about ten? I mean, tonight. It's nearly five in the morning."

"Tonight then. I'll be there."

He kissed her and went out.

Chapter Four

*I*n this hour or so before dawn, the coastal highway was practically deserted. Mostly the traffic would consist, as Ballard knew, of the few brave winter vacationers who wanted to drop their fishing lines at first light. And then there would be a few party-goers, home-bound stragglers like himself.

But Ballard gave only a minimum attention to the road. He was thinking that, after nearly a month in the hospital, he was about to sleep for the first time in his own bed. No matter how pleasant and efficient the doctors and the staff personnel, the sick and the dying were depressing and the cool austerity and impersonality of a hospital were far from cheerful. So that there was some small comfort in returning to the cozy and familiar atmosphere of his own beach apartment.

He had been discharged from the hospital just before noon the preceding day and he had gone directly to the radio station. But Ray Sawyer, his general manager, was taking an extended lunch break with an important client and he didn't feel like explaining anything to Pete Mulford, his program director. Ray was not only his manager but a close personal friend and knew most of the facts. Mulford was strictly an employee — a capable PD, but certainly not a confidant. So after going over his mail and telling Pat Hooper, his secretary, that — Yes, thanks, he was feeling fine after the "accident," — he left for the day. Ray was running the business smoothly and somehow Ballard couldn't get his mind oh it. The transition was too swift and his spirit wasn't going to return to him until the affair of the Gold Reef Bar was burned out of his mind with action.

There had been a cold snap a few days before with the temperature getting down to 55° — a real horror of an Arctic freeze for southern Florida in January. But when he left the station, it was in the seventies again. The sun was bright with temperate heat rays for slow tanning and he decided to restore some color to his face and body; take a swim and think things out. Mostly he wanted to kill time until the Gold Reef closed and he could force some information from the owner the police had called Beef Costigan.

He had baked a few hours on the beach, washed the feeling of atrophy from mind and body, cooked his own supper, read an entire paperback novel, napped and then it was time to have a little chat with Costigan. . . .

Now, at 5 a.m., as he was passing through Holly-wood Beach, he was speculating about the man he had seen watching him over the railing from the second floor of Gould's place. Paula Schaeffer's jealous lover? Unlikely. If the man were Paula's lover, she would hardly be downstairs smooching with someone else. Not unless she was an idiot. And she was far from that. No, probably the man was another of Gould's flunkies. Well, the guy hadn't learned much from what was said and he hadn't seen the best of what little was done, so, for the moment, it didn't matter. One day the whole picture would be put together and his place in the puzzle would come to light.

Even a distant and foggy glimpse of that picture didn't look good. Solid citizens with legitimate enterprises didn't go around sapping and brass-knuckling people in bars and didn't consort with half-world types like Sharp Nose and Fish Eyes. It was Ballard's bet that Gould didn't consort with them, either, except on special occasions. The rest of the time he probably kept them hidden in that same closet where he hid whatever were his real activities — the ones that took him to Chicago. No, on the surface, Gould appeared a smoothie and his operation smelled of flowers growing over a sewer.

But if he was such a smart boy, what made him loose his goons on a perfect stranger, damn near kill him over the small issue of a song played once too often? Ballard guessed that it was a thoughtless act based on a psychological quirk of Gould's personality. His cruelty was obviously native. He probably enjoyed meting out physical punishment in comparative safety from reprisal. That was part of it. The rest must be a distorted ego which would not be crossed on the smallest of things. For probably it was Gould who had sent Sharp Nose to tell him to "knock it off," in the first place.

It was a dangerous situation, thought Ballard. He had about as much chance of getting at Gould as a man on a bicycle attacking an armored car. And in trying, he might take more than a beating next time. He might be another of those mysterious people in Dade County, like judge William J. Hoffsteader, who just disappear from the face of the earth and are never heard from again.

Sensibly, the best plan would be to forget the whole thing. He could chalk up a tangible loss of seven hundred and fifty dollars. And an intangible loss in time. But time was money. He would have been seeing people, selling very tangible commercial time to them on his radio station. Estimate a minimum possible sale of spot commercials amounting to five hundred dollars. And a maximum of two thousand for a contracted. program. So split the difference and call it a thousand. With hospital bill, a total of seventeen hundred and fifty dollars. In civil court, the amount of damages he could collect above expenses for physical and mental shock, general discomfort, inconvenience, etc., were inestimable — especially since a jury or judge would take into consideration the wealth of the defendant. Much would depend on the skill of his own attorney. But lump tangibles and intangibles together and Gould would be getting off practically scot-free with a judgment against him of five thousand dollars.

And there were no witnesses — just Costigan. The customer who phoned the police didn't see a thing. He came in after it was over, when Costigan "was about to call the police myself." Ha! And Ballard figured that having thought the situation over, Costigan would be more afraid of Gould than of him and would promptly deny to the police any knowledge of Gould. And he would stick with his story to the end.

So he could chalk up a minimum loss of five thousand and the satisfaction of vengeance. The safe, the intelligent thing was to do just that.

But the truth was that whatever the risk, it was a loss he was not ready to take. Not the financial loss, but the loss of fiber in himself. Unless he trampled Gould and his we'll-hold-'im-while-you-hit-'im-boss pals, he would never be able to move about in his world with any confidence or pride. Something of character, of toughness, of a sense of rightness and integrity would drain out of him. Others might only feel it. But for all time he would know it. And in effect he would be condoning the right of three goons to walk into a bar, beat a man half to death on a whim and get away with it — go completely unchallenged. And that he was not about to do.

And, though it was an afterthought, it was still true that not since Julie had he met anyone as intriguing as Paula Schaeffer. But whether he would ever respect her was going to depend on proving that her sweet little story was fact — not act.

In any case, Gould had made a bigger mistake than he could imagine. He had dropped a mere pebble in a small pond. But as far as Ballard was concerned, the circles from that pebble were going to widen and widen until they became waves that washed to shore all the dirty, slimy dregs that must lie on the muddy bottom of Gould's surface-pretty empire.

He was thinking about the Tropic Owl and the many clubs like it with nebulous ownership, when he first became aware that there was a lone car behind him and that this car had been following him far some time.

He wasn't anxious to lose the car. On the contrary, he was anxious to keep it, identify it and whoever rode in it. There was a possibility that this could be done if he made some cagey turns and continued to play the innocent he had really been a minute or two before.

He took the same route that he would normally cover, swinging west to Dasria and the Federal Highway, they north again to Fort Lauderdale, turning east on the Seventeenth Street Causeway to the beach.

He drove at a normal clip and kept a careful watch. The car hung well back, allowing other vehicles to interpose from time to time but always maintaining the necessary visual contact.

Instead of remaining on the beach road and taking

the drawbridge over the Intracoastal Waterway as usual, Ballard wheeled left a quarter mile from it and entered a housing development area with which he was familiar. Watching, he observed that the car did not make the turn but went on by slowly. Logically, the driver must have figured that if he followed at this point, he would give himself away.

Knowing that his tail could still spot his next change of direction, Ballard now tooled right — into a dead-end street. His lights would be visible between houses. But unless the tail had pinpoint knowledge of the area, he would not guess that the street terminated at a canal.

The rest was quite simple. At the end of the narrow street there was a loop, a turn-a-round. At the neck of the loop, left side, there was a small house with a FOR SALE sign staked into the lawn. The sign gave the phone number of a real estate office. The house was empty, as Ballard well knew, because just before his abrupt trip to the hospital, he had inspected it with the thought that he might trade his co-op apartment on the beach for a house on a canal. Luckily for his present purpose, the house had not yet been sold.

Now he drove to the center of the loop, shoved in reverse and backed into the driveway of the empty house until he was well hidden. This done, he doused his lights and waited, motor on.

In less than two minutes, a car approached, came to the loop and began the turn. It was a long, smooth hunk of canvas and metal — a Lincoln Continental — ten thousand dollars' worth of get-up-and-go that wasn't going anywhere at all for the present. Because before it could gun away, Ballard had bolted from the drive and closed the loop at the neck. The Lincoln was neatly blocked.

Only one person slunk out of the big car and he was

in shadow behind the lights. Ballard jumped out, pocketing the keys and approaching swiftly in a flanking movement that would keep him out of the glare.

A man ran between houses, disappeared. Ballard followed. They came face to face, or at least, shadow to shadow, as Ballard rounded a corner of the nearest house.

The man stepped out from the wall in a position of crouching defense. It could be the guy who had leaned over the balcony of Gould's second floor. In the darkness, there way a vague similarity of build. Ballard asked no questions but moved in far a quick knockdown.

He feinted with a left and swung a beautiful right that never connected. Instead, his wrist and arm were caught in steel-hard claws and he west sailing over the man's shoulder, landing on his back with a meaty, bruising thump.

Before he could roll over and came shakily to his knees, he heard the door of the Lincoln slam. And as he watched, the Continental backed, shooed over the sidewalk, maneuvered around a palm onto someone's lawn, cleared the Pontiac and dropped back to the street, disappearing wig a thrust of power.

"You dumb bastard," muttered Ballard as he brushed himself off and began to hobble to his car, "why didn't you think of that in the first place?"

Chapter Five

*T*he Tropic Owl is a cream-colored building of stone and glass situated at the ocean on the southern fringe of Pompano Beach. It has a peculiar and striking architecture. At the base, the housing for the lower building, it is square. But the three-storied structure rising from the center of the base is completely round, forming a wide tower somewhat like that of a lighthouse.

The ground floor is merely a reception area and lounge, though behind this there is a large kitchen which sends food aloft on dumb-waiters, a storeroom or two and the office of the manager. Floors above can be reached by means of a carpeted, spiraling ramp or by elevator. The first floor contains a bar and lounge with tables located around the windowed circumference. These windows are huge squares which angle inward and reach to the ceiling, the identical arrangement of glass being carried out on the floors above. From all but the extreme west side of the structure, there is an ascendingly beautiful view of the ocean with beach and coconut palms in the foreground.

In the first-floor cocktail lounge, the lights are so dim that electric candles can be seen on the tables from the road. In the center of the room there is a Hammond electric organ played skillfully by a pert little redhead. Most of the songs are ballads which she croons over a PA system in a sultry voice. But as the hour grows late and the tempo of the night accelerates, the songs take on a beat, a bluesy, suggestive quality. As in most rooms of the type, the atmosphere contains a purposeful undertone of sensuality.

The second floor caters strictly to those gourmets who prefer their dining with no more distraction than a three-piece ensemble discreetly playing light classics, melodies in the range between long and short hair.

On the third floor there is also fine cuisine but the whole design is for supper-club entertainment and the room does not open until nine in the evening. This room has only a small service bar; the remaining space is devoted to a circular dance floor around which tables are placed and a semicircular podium for eight-piece orchestra. During the three nightly shows, the entertainers use the dance floor. This gives them close contact with the audience and creates a feeling of intimate participation.

Altogether, the Tropic Owl is a masterpiece of lush splendor, a place where moods change on every floor and the whims of its patrons have been carefully anticipated. But for this, they pay dearly.

Gil Ballard arrived under the supper-room dome of the Tropic Owl at ten o'clock. Paula Schaeffer, still wearing the same white dress, or one just like it, as though this was required costume for the job, stood by the entrance to the room. She greeted people with a gracious smile, consulted reservations, summoned waiters and occasionally made herself a personal escort to some chosen table. It seemed improbable that anyone could find their way without escort for the room was two shades darker than the Top of the Mark at midnight. And that's about as dark as you can get without cane and seeing-eye dog.

"Hi," she said, flashing a pearly smile in the gloom. "I wasn't sure whether you were coming. But I held a table."

"Ringside, of course."

"No, as a matter of fact, from this little table you can't see anything but me. It has one advantage, though — it's for free."

"Good. I'll take it with me when I leave."

She Laughed. "You'd never get away with it. The bulge would show under your coat. Besides, you know very well I mean the house will pick up the tab."

"I'm glad. Because I think it would be too heavy for me to pick up by myself," he said. And thought, Gould, old buddy, this will be your first but not your last unwitting payment.

"All right, truce," said Paula, chuckling. "Now follow me."

They didn't have far to go. The two-place table was just a few steps away, close to the entrance and Paula. However, it was by a window with a fine display of ocean. And the room was small enough for easy viewing of the show.

"Seriously," she said when he was seated, "I could put you up close, but you might feel a little conspicuous alone."

"Amusingly," he said, "this is great. Can you join me?"

"Maybe later for a quick one. Not now. Much too

busy. But I'll come and stand innocently close so I can chat with you once in a while.''

''Okay. What time is the first show?''

She looked at her watch, straining in the dark. ''Any minute now. After this set.'' She peered over her shoulder. ''Damn! I've got to run. Customers. See you in a few minutes.'' She scurried off.

Ballard told the waiter who came in a moment to hover over him that — No, he did not desire dinner but would have a double Manhattan, posthaste.

Meanwhile, the orchestra, resplendent in red jackets and white trousers, brought a mambo to a crashing climax, then chorused rhythmically,

> *"Won't you please sit down — have a drink?*
> *We'll be right back in just a wink,*
> *And if you have to go,*
> *Then go and don't be slow,*
> *It's nearly time to start our show,*

And they weren't kidding. In less than a minute the Band leader announced on the tail-end of a fanfare of trumpets that this was a moment fat extreme jubilation because here now was the ''Piece of Resistance — Maxine and Her Playmates!''

Maxine appeared in spotlight from nowhere. She wore extremely high-heeled shoes, gold toreador pants that fit like wet silk, and an abbreviated jacket of jet with gold sequins. The jacket missed meeting the pants by about a foot and revealed a generous portion of pink-white midriff with matching navel. The jacket was cut in a deep V so victorious that the abundant swell of her breasts was almost a complete winner over the skimpy material.

Though she appeared much taller in those high

heels, Ballard had little trouble identifying the blonde Maxine as the girl clinching with the man on the couch at Gould's house.

Now she bowed dangerously low to an ovation of sighs and whistles. As she straightened, the spotlight picked up three men bouncing on stage, carrying, respectively, string bass, accordion, and drums.

Someone brought a chair for the drummer and, with the bass fiddle player acting as comic MC, the show got underway.

The act was a combination of top-notch vocal harmony (solos by Maxine) and smutty, though artful, byplay with Maxine acting as foil.

There were sweet songs, tempo songs and beat instrumentals featuring drum and bass fiddle. The show was belly-laugh funny, alternately wild and sentimental. It had pace. The audience loved it.

During it, Paula stood near and once she said, "How do you like Maxine?"

"She's the coolest, dad," said Gil. "A real professional."

"She should be," said Paula. "For three thousand a week."

"My God! Does she have a day job to make ends meet?"

"She has to split some of the take with the boys, of course," said Paula. "But she comes away with the lion's share."

"Lioness'," said Gil.

"If you had come a couple of minute's earlier," said Paula smiling, "you would have met her at the house this morning. She and two of the Playmates dropped by."

"I suppose she's one of Gould's favorites," said Ballard cautiously. She looked like someone's favorite on a fast track.

"Oh, yes," said Paula. "More than that. Russ brought her from Chicago. She hinted that they've been thick for years. And don't ask me if it was business. I don't think she likes me and she keeps what she knows to herself."

"I've never found two good-looking women who liked each other very much," he said. "Anyway, I want to meet her."

"Oh?"

"Just curious." But he was more than curious. He was down right anxious to meet anyone who knew Russ Gould well. With the least help from Paula, he could play the intimate-friend-and-business-associate part to the hilt — until Gould returned. But to pump information from Maxine, he would have to be very careful.

"Well, listen," said Paula, throwing him into the breads with pretended indifference. "I'm going to be tied up after the show, but Maxine will be free for about an hour and a half. I could introduce you and you two could kill time over a drink."

"This single routine does get dull. Sure you won't mind, Paula?"

"Not at all. I have nothing against Maxine. She's always good for a tough. I'll fix it up."

But when they were introduced, he didn't think Maxine was going to be good for a laugh at all. When she turned that stage personality off, she seemed quiet, subdued. And in some strange way, a little frightened.

She approached with a careful little step, weaving around tables in the dark. Out of spotlight, her nature seemed to diminish, especially since she walked with a slight stoop, shoulders hunched together almost as if she were cold in that tropic cloister.

"Max, this is a close business friend of Russ

Gould's. Gil Ballard."

"How do you do?" she said almost shyly, while beading toward him and displaying mammary glands, caliber 38, pointed like bullets of the same caliber and almost as persuasive.

"Gil is doing a single tonight," said Paula, "and he was wondering if you'd like to have a drink or two with him between shows."

"Love it," said Maxine. "Any friend of Russ's . . ." She sat down and studied her crimson nails.

"Have fun," said Paula. "Check with you later." She departed.

"I really ought to change," said Maxine with a quick downward glance at her seminakedness.

She stands up there for all the world to see and now suddenly she's shy with one man in the dark, thought Ballard. You never know. But she wasn't so shy on that much the other night . . .

"Don't bother to change," he said. "I caught the act."

She laughed nervously. "So you're a good friend of Russ's. He never told me about you. But then it's a big com — it's big business he deals in, and there are a lot of his people I don't meet or ever hear about."

He was sure she was going to say combine, not company. "Well," he explained, "Russ has been keeping me under wraps." And wasn't that the truth! "You might say I have a very special function."

He had used the remark as a dodge, but it seemed to alarm her unreasonably. Her eyes grew wide and she chewed on hex lip. She had exceedingly smooth skin, baked with a beautiful tan that didn't disappear on the way down to the junction of the V. Her cheekbones were high, descending to intriguing hollows. Her mouth was small, the lips heavy, her chin narrow and, at the same time, nicely rounded. The face was a composite of angularity and fullness that made it intense and attractive.

It was not a hard face, though there was a worldliness, a shrewd watchfulness in the slate-blue eyes. And though she wasn't working at it now, she was a dynamo of sex appeal. Ballard guessed that she was close to thirty.

"What do you mean — you have a special function?" she was saying is a guarded tone.

"I can't tell you," said Ballard solemnly. "I guess yon know that, Maxine." He had decided to continue on the same tack, employing mystery as a tool to uncover mystery.

She nodded. "Of course. I'm sorry. Who should know the ways of Russ Gould better than I?"

"No one," he said. "I can't think of anyone who should know better."

"Ross told you about me?" Again she seemed startled, unnerved.

The waiter came to take their order and they were silent until he had gone.

"What were you saying?" asked Ballard casually.

"I wanted to know if Russ had told you about me?"

"Sure. Sure, he told me."

"Everything?"

He smiled. "Well now, that depends on what you mean. He told me all the important things — Chicago, how he trusted you, things like that. And, of course, that you were very close."

"Were close?"

"Well —"

He had guessed correctly because she said, "So he doesn't think he can trust me any more."

"I didn't say that. Not at all."

"Yes, but that's what you meant."

She watched him with a breathless intensity.

"Well, you know, Maxine, if the shoe fits —"

"Please!" she said. "Don't frighten me. Just tell me the truth. I can take it. I'd rather know. I have to know."

"I wouldn't worry about it," he said. "I wouldn't take it too seriously. You know Russ — he's changeable."

"I suppose he sent you to watch me while he was gone."

"If he did, do you think I would tell you?"

She chewed on one bright nail nervously. Her face was expressionless, drained of its individuality. "Naturally," she said in a bitter, faraway, voice, "you wouldn't tell me."

Ballard felt sorry for her. The poor kid was scared and he wasn't helping at all. He was tightening the nut. But was there a better way to get information than to pretend you had it all? Later he would find a way to ease up on her. But right now he dominated. She was so frightened she couldn't see that if he were watching her, if he posed a threat, he wouldn't be sitting there talking to her.

He let the silence between them gather its own tension and looked down from the window. Palm trees sprang upward from the sand and a warm breeze toyed with their green-mop hairdos. At the edge of the beach, waves broke gently and receded in a white froth of perpetual motion. There was a restrained wildness in the scene and a timeless rhythm that was somnolent.

"Tell me about Paula," he said. "I met her only last night. She seems green. What's her game? Is she on the inside?"

Now if she said something like "Inside? What do you mean?" he was licked. But her face lost some of its wariness in the change of subject and she answered,

"Paula? On the inside? No. She's still way out on the edge. She doesn't even smell smoke. But she will. Russ will corrupt her, too."

He gave hex a sharp, purposeful look.

She put her hand to her mouth. "I'm sorry. I shouldn't have said that. I'm jumpy tonight."

"That's all right," he said. "I know the score. And school's out for now. So you can speak freely with me." But there was a core of hardness in his voice when he said, "You didn't tell her anything, did you?"

"Me? My God, no. Not word one. She doesn't even know that Russ and I were married in the good old days when he was climbing and he needed me."

He kept the surprise from his face. But Maxine was twice important now. He was going to squeeze her dry. He was going to needle her until she was ready to scream. And then he was going to go soft and pliable and when the relief closed around her like a warm bath, she would open her pretty mouth and the words would pour out. He would take those words and put them together and, build a club of them that would beat Gould down more finally than *he* had been beaten on a night almost a month ago. He was certain now that he was going to ruin Russell Gould and Company.

It was a dirty trick to play on Maxine. But the whole game was dirty and she might come through with a permanent release in the end.

"You did the right thing, Max," he said. "You played it smart. If Russ wants to take Paula in, he'll do it when he's ready."

"He may take her," she said with a sardonic smile, "but I doubt if he'll ever take her in. You can't put claws on lamb and call it cat."

"You hate her, don't you?" he said.

"No, I don't hate her. Not any more than I do all the

others. And, kiddo, there's been a string. It's a big stable."

"Yeah. Sure it is. But give a stallion plenty of rein and he might wander home again. Know what I mean?"

She shook her head. "I don't think so. Before Paula I had hope. But not now."

"You think he's serious this time?"

"I know it. I can tell by the way he's playing her — the patient approach, no crowding and a nice, flower-bedded trap closing slowly."

"You've got a point there," he said. "But don't forget you're skimming the cream off three grand a week. And what's she getting? Peanuts!"

"Listen," said Maxine, leaning forward. "Don't kid yourself. I net eighteen hundred a week because I'm worth it. I draw the suckers and the suckers pay — plenty. Russ knows that. I could get as much, maybe more from some other club. The boys are good. But they're just props. I could get another bunch together, maybe not quite as sharp, and still make it pay off. Because the customers are buying sex whether they know it or not. Russ is an operator either side of the line. He gets his money's worth."

"You've got the picture," he said. "You know Russ, all right."

"Where is Russ now?" she said.

He simply looked at her coldly.

"Then will you tell me when he'll be back?"

He stared her down.

"I see," she said. "But while he's gone you're watching the chicken coop."

He didn't answer. He glanced at his watch. No use overworking a good thing. Time and silence would conspire against her. He gulped his drink.

"I've got to beat it," he said. "I'm on company time.

Understand? But I'll see you around, Max. You can count on it.''

Nervousness returned to her in a flurry of anxiety. The skin tightened around her cheekbones. She leaned forward and covered his hand on the table with her own. ''Don't go,'' she pleaded. ''Not yet. Please. I want to talk to you. There are things I have to know.''

He withdrew his hand from under heir. ''Don't give me that about things you have to know,'' he said. ''You know all you're going to know. You think I want to put my head an the block, too?''

''Oh, Jesus,'' she said hoarsely. ''Oh, Christ. Give me a break, Gil. You seem like a nice guy. You're not a machine like Needle Nose and The Ox. Give me a break and I'll see that you never regret it.''

His mind raced. Needle Nose and The Ox. The names should be funny — but he wasn't laughing. They would be the two clowns with Gould at the bar. The pieces were falling is place.

''Listen,'' he hissed. ''You keep your mouth shut! Don't be passing names where people might hear.''

''All right,'' she said abjectly. ''I'm sorry. But what about it?''

''What about what?''

''Giving me a break. I told you you'd never regret it.''

''Never regret it,'' he mimicked. ''Come on now, Maxine. What have you got to offer me? Money? I've got plenty. The kind of cash I'm looking for you haven't seen yet.''

She glanced down. Her eyes came up slowly. Her hand stole over his again and this time he let it rest there. ''There are things besides money,'' she said softly. ''There are things that can make you forget all about money and Russ Gould and the others.''

"Yeah," he said. "For a couple of hours. And then where am I?"

"There are hours and there are whole nights," she said. "Lots of hours and lots of nights. Anyway, I'm not going to ask you for anything but a little advice. And besides, who would ever know?"

He pretended to be thoughtful. "I won't promise anything," he said.

"I'm not asking you to. Just let me talk to you. In private."

"When?"

"The last show breaks at one-thirty."

"Where?"

"I'll give you my address."

"You think I don't know it?"

She swallowed. "About two, then?"

"Let's play it safe," he said. "You come to my place. After, the last show. I'll be waiting."

"How do I get there?"

He told her. Then he said, "And listen, don't even hint it to Paula. Don't trust anyone. Was she expecting you to take her home?"

"No. I was going to do a few late joints with the boys and so Carl drove her. I think he's waiting outside."

"Good. See you about two then."

He dropped a bill on the table for the tip. Then got up and walked away.

"You have a ride borne?" he asked Paula at the exit.

"Yes. The chauffeur brought me. But I could tell him to go on. I wasn't sure if —"

"I'd like to stay," he said. "But it's a week night and I have to hit the studio early in the morning. New show on the board and I west to help shove it off to a good start. Forgive me?"

"Of course."

"Maybe tomorrow night. Saturday at the latest."

"Call me and let me know."

"I will. And thanks for the free-loading. One thing more. I think for personal reasons Russ would rather you didn't discuss my part in his setup with Maxine. You don't know anything about me or what I do. Okay?"

"Well, it's practically the truth. But I won't say a word."

"She may try to pump you. I think she has an idea I'm going to take over the club."

"Are you?"

"Never can tell. It's more or less in my line."

"I still won't tell her a thing."

"Thanks. 'Night, Paula."

He went out. The air was fresh and clean and warm and he was feeling good. He had groped his way along, using neat timing, applying pressure at the right points. Maxine was ripe and she had made it easy for him to fall into the part naturally. In a grim sort of way, it was fun. But he could sense the danger uncovering itself and he would not be lulled to sleep with overconfidence.

There was a sea of cars hubcap to hubcap on the parking lot. He spotted his, but kept on looking. There were several Lincoln Continentals. Only one was convertible and boasted a chauffeur.

He walked up an aisle two cars away and took a good look. Even with the gray uniform and the peak cap, he knew that the chauffeur was the man who had been watching over the rail at Gould's house.

He went around and approached from the rear on the driver's side. He leaned on the door and watched the man's mouth gape open.

"You're a clever boy at jujitsu, Carl," he said. "But don't try to follow me again. Next time you might have a bad accident."

He grabbed the visor and gave the cap a downward yank over the man's face.

Whistling, he went on to his own car and drove off.

Chapter Six

"How did you get those scars on your face?" said Maxine. "I didn't notice them before."

She had arrived breathless and eager at five minutes to two. She had not bothered to change her costume, cloaking herself with a mandarin jacket which she removed rather obviously when Gil began to mix drinks behind the portable bar. Now he was offering a stinger across the Formica top and she was leaning toward him, smiling, inspecting his face.

"You ask too many questions," he said. He was having difficulty playing it cold while watching the warm hills of her breasts mounting from the sequined jacket to nudge the bar.

"Don't get sore, honey," she said. "I was just curious."

He lighted her cigarette and picked up his drink, sipping it. "Well, it's no secret." His fingers touched the thin line where his lip had been ripped open. "I got into a brawl one night. The guy who was hitting me must have been afraid he'd skin his knuckles. They were all brass.'' He doused the overhead light, came from behind the bar and eased onto the sofa.

She followed, saying, "You look like you can handle yourself, Gil. I'll bet you conked him good." She blew a cloud of smoke toward the one lighted lamp in the room and a gray haze drifted upward around the bulb.

"No," he said. "It got dark there for a while and when the lights went on he was gone. But someday I'll meet him again."

"And then?"

"I know a good plastic surgeon I could send him to."

She felt his arm. "My God, I'd hate to be on the wrong side of all that power," she said reverently.

He was silent.

"Do you muscle for Russ?"

"I told you not to ask so many questions."

"I thought you were going to let down that barrier a little for me."

"Okay, okay. Give me time. This whole thing stinks. It makes me nervous."

"Even if Russ knew," she said, "I don't think he'd care. Not now."

"Sure. It wouldn't bother him at all. He could catch us on the mat and he wouldn't care. If the situation was different."

She set down her drink and said in an awed tone, "What do you mean?"

He twirled the ice in his glass until the silence got on his own nerves. "Tell me this," he said. "Did you and Russ have a beef?"

"Did he tell you that?"

"Not in so many words."

Words, words, he thought. I'm juggling them like hand grenades.

"Well, we did," she said. "Not one of those real violent flare-ups. Those I can handle. But a quiet sort of thing. He was so polite. He gave me the weeps."

"What was it all about?"

"You don't know?"

"That part, he didn't tell me."

She studied the tip of her cigarette. "How do I know I can trust you, Gil? How do I know it won't leak back?"

"You don't. What did you expect, an affidavit? If you're afraid of me, then keep it to yourself."

"I can't. I need you. And yet I can't trust anyone. Not any more."

He waited.

"Oh, hell," she said. "What difference does it make? I can't get in much deeper. . . . Some things were said. They weren't pretty. And I happened to overhear them."

"Well, so what?"

"I was out on the beach. About a month ago. I was living with Russ at the time. We were very chummy. We haven't been married for about five years. But we were always close. Don't ask me why, but he never got over me. Always thought I was pretty special. And he was talking about making it legal again, providing I let him run free whenever he wanted to. I was going along with him because with Russ there's no choice.

"Anyway, as I said, I was out on the beach this day, toasting up under the sun. Russ was in the den. Needle Nose and The Ox were in there with him, guzzling. You know them, don't you?"

"Hell, yes. I know those clowns. Too damn well."

"I can't stand either one of them," she said. "They're sick. And they make *me* sick. But I wasn't sure if you knew them because, except on rare occasions,

Russ must keep them down in some cellar where none of his legitimate friends can see them. I don't think there are half a dozen who know about them and what they do. Just the top brass." She gave him a look.

"Well?" he said.

"Okay, I won't ask questions. But to go on. I figured that if Ox and Needle were there at all — and in broad daylight — something big was up. I knew Russ wouldn't tell me anything. He never talks about them. And I was curious. But not so I couldn't stand it. I just stayed out on the beach and forget about it.

"In about an hour, I couldn't take any more sun and I came on up to the house. You probably know that the den is around by the swimming pool."

"Uh-huh."

"And there's a little shower there against the wall, to get the sand off. I turned it on and I was washing my feet. I heard voices but I didn't pay much attention. Not then. I sat down on the grass to dry myself with a towel. I was right under a window to the den and the window was open. That's when I began to hear things. And once I got started listening, I couldn't stop. It was that bad."

"Well, sure," he said. "We're not playing bingo, you know."

"Yes, but this was different. I don't care if they make book around the world and run clip joints and super call-girl blinds and even bleed the unions. There'll always be as many takers as there are suckers. And the Syndicate stays in business because it pays off on the other side of the line and keeps a fairly clean nose. I mean stick-ups, things like that. But listening to them I was cold all over — right in the sun."

"What then? Did Russ catch you?"

"No. If I'd kept my mouth shut he'd never have known I was listening. But later I had to go and tell him what I thought about it. I was furious. And I was scared, too. I got so wound up I even threatened him. And all the time he just sat there smiling and nodding and saying, 'You shouldn't have been listening, Max. But you were, Max. And you know, that's bad for you, Max. So you better go somewhere and think about what you heard. Think about it real carefully and what it means, Max. What it could mean to you. And then you come back wearing a zipper on your mouth. And that god-damn zipper better have a big lock. And no key. No key at all, Max.'

"That's all he said to me. That's all he ever said to me about it. But he changed after that. He was cool. I couldn't get to him at all. Next thing you know he told me it might be better if I took my own place for a while. He got an apartment lined up for me and I found myself eased right into it. Then Paula came along and after that he didn't even drop in to see me any more."

"Well," he said, "it could get worse, you know."

"It did. It got worse right away. That Carl began to follow me. He made no bones at all about it. And then I would look out my window when I came home and there would be a strange car parked there. Or a man I didn't recognize leaning against a tree, looking up at me. I have the feeling that I'm being watched twenty-four hours a day."

"It wouldn't surprise me, Max. Now, what was it you heard?"

"If you can't guess, you're not going to find out from me," she said. "I'd have to know you a lot better and a lot longer. For all I know they sent you as a decoy, to see if I'd pass the test."

"Never mind," he said. "I don't have to guess." The hell he didn't. He had to guess it all the way, though now it was unfolding enough for him to get the general idea.

He had started out to revenge a beating and he had stumbled into a combine of evil. Evil too deep to imagine. And now there were questions he had to ask and couldn't ask. How could you get answers you were supposed to have?

"You know?" she said. "You know what they were planning and you don't care?"

"Sure, I care. I don't like it any better than you do. But I'm only one guy. How can I stop orders that come down from the top?"

"All right," she said. "So what are the orders for me? The firing squad at dawn?"

He didn't answer.

She grabbed him by the shoulders and began to shake him. "Say something!" she shouted. "For God's sake, say something! I'm on the list, is that it? They're going to kill me. I knew it. I knew it!" She leaned against him and began to sob in soft gulps of sound.

He couldn't take any more of it, no matter what was to be gained. He put his arm around her. "Don't worry, Max," he said. "They're not going to hurt you. Whatever they've got in mind, I'll figure a way out for you. I won't let them touch you."

She straightened, drying her eyes. "You'll help me?" she said pathetically.

He nodded. "I'll help you. I'll do what I can."

"Why should you help me? Why should you be on my side? I haven't done anything for you. Not yet."

"Because," he said, "they've gone too far. I've got soave conscience left. And I draw the line at killing."

She studied him. "I thought so. You didn't look the type. Right from the beginning I had a hunch you'd help me. But you said it, honey. You put it right when you said you're only one man. How can you stop a steam roller?"

"I don't know," he said. "That's something I don't know yet. But I'm going to think about it. I'm going to try to come up with something."

"For instance?"

"The only way you can stop force," he said carefully, "is with superior force."

"And where are you going to get that force? There's nothing bigger than the combine."

"Yes, there is," he said.

She looked at him in amazement. "Are you talking about the police?"

He nodded.

She jumped up, crossed the room to the bar, turned. "You're crazy!" she said. "You're out of your mind. If you meant what you said, you just committed suicide."

"There's one way it could be done," he said. "Only one sure way."

"How?"

"If you told everything you know and I told everything I know. And we mold back it up with evidence. Then they'd clean out the whole nest."

"You are crazy," she said. "If they left even a little corner of that nest, the rats would swarm out and kill us. Anywhere on earth. And why do you want to cut off the hand that's feeding you?"

"I told you. It's gone too far. I've had it. I want out."

She fumbled behind the bar and found a battle of bourbon and a glass. She poured the glass a quarter full. Her hand was shaking.

"That won't mix well," he said.

"I don't care." She drank it all, made a face and poured another. "Listen," she said. "You make me almost as nervous as they do. Can that talk about the police, will you?"

"Think about it, Max. Don't hurry. Just think about

it.''

She shook her head, drank the bourbon, gulped. "I've already thought about it too long. Even if we could get away with it, the Syndicate has long arms. They reach right inside most of the police departments around the country. And the arms have hands. And the hands open and they drop money. Big wads of it that shut mouths and keep the prowl cars in their stables. Besides, you could be just setting me up for a trap. No thanks.''

She leaned bark against the bar. Her eyes had become hard.

This one's going to be tough to crack, he thought. It's going to take time. Somehow he would have to gain her confidence. "But you want me to help you?" he said.

"Oh, God, yes, Gil. But some other way. Some other way."

"All right," he said. "I'll figure something."

She came over to him and kissed him. "You know what I like about you? You're willing to help me, but you don't ask anything in return. You haven't made a pass at me yet."

He smiled. "Give me time," he said.

"Sure," she said. "I'll give you lots of time. Starting now."

She stood tall with her shoulders back. The sensual fire that was hers on stage spread through her face and body. She pivoted. "Do you see any reason why the customers should get so upset? When they can't touch the merchandise?"

"I see lots of reasons," he said.

Her smile was sly. "I know of two good ones, anyway," she said. Her hands toyed with the hook that fastened the jacket together. Suddenly she wrenched it apart.

She wore nothing underneath. The beautiful tan

ended abruptly and the swelling cones of her breasts were startlingly white. In contrast, the peaks were dark circles with extended nipples.

She came toward him, stood over him. Slowly she pulled his head against her. With one hand she undid the gold toreador pants and slipped out of them, taking the high heeled shoes with them. A rustle of sound and the black lace panties were next.

She was naked.

"I didn't see a bedroom," she muttered.

"You will," he said. "You will."

*T*hey were lying in the dark close together and she was stroking his back. "You're much man," she said. "Much, much. I didn't want to make love to you this way and like you at the same time. But I do. And even now I can't relax. There's a chill in me that won't thaw out. A warm body next to me, the hat sun, a scalding bath — nothing will make the shiver that's in me go away."

"Max," he said softly. "Believe me, I want to help you. In the name of God, I want to help you. What was it you heard?"

There was a silence. "I heard — I heard them planning to —"

"Planning what, Max?"

"Planning murder."

Chapter Seven

*D*etective Lieutenant Kohler frowned behind his desk. He looked up at Ballard, squinting behind the gauze of cigarette smoke.

"So then you took her home, is that it? But after she told you there was going to be a killing or there had been one, she clammed up."

"That's right," Ballard answered. "I think the poor kid was sorry she said that much. She doesn't trust anyone and you can't blame her."

Lieutenant Kohler sank back in his chair and passed a look. to Detective Sergeant Rubison who sat an a corner of the desk, listening in silence. Kohler was a tall lean man in his early forties. His dark hair receded from a high forehead. He had a strong, angular fate with pocked skin around the cheekbones. His gray eyes under bushy brows had the cool, distant look of having seen too much, too often. The other, Rubisan, was younger by a good five years, and shorter. He had light red hair, a blunt bulldog face and a chunky muscularity. His brown eyes seemed always a little amused. He was one of the two officers who had questioned Ballard at the hospital.

"Whatta you think?" said Kohler, still looking at Rubisan.

"It smells a little ripe," said Rubisan. "But not ripe enough. We'll need more than a bunch of second-hand stories to move on it."

"My God," said Ballard disgustedly. "Do you need affidavits and samples of spilled blood?"

Kohler nodded, tapped a pencil on the desk. "Practically," he said. "Yes, practically."

"It seems to me I've heard all this before," said Ballard. "When I was in the hospital."

"I know," said Kohler. "I know how you feel. We run into this all the time. Everyone is in a hurry. They want action. Now! And by God, there are times like this when I wish we could throw away the book. But we have people to answer to upstairs just like anyone else. And while the rules are slow and they let some fish slip through the net now and then, the truth is that most of the time they pay off. This isn't the fire department. Unfortunately we can't run every time someone yells smoke and then mark it up to another false alarm at the city's expense. Because when we run, someone usually gets hurt in one way or another. Just the minute we haul some citizen into a police station, he begins to hurt. And we damn well have to have aces or the whole thing backfires. You see what I mean?"

Ballard got up from his chair, crossed the room, turned, came back to lean over the desk. "Take a look at these scars, Lieutenant. How do you like those aces!"

"All right," said Kohler. "That's the kind of thing we can work on. But what happens? This morning when you called in we went over and dug Costigan out of bed.

So what does he say? He don't know anyone by the name of Gould and to his knowledge this Gould was never in his bar. Furthermore, he never admitted anything to you because he's never seen you since they carted you away in an ambulance." He held up his hand as Ballard's mouth worked over an angry objection. "Never mind. I know what you're gonna say. Well, the sonofabitch has a sneaky look about him and I don't believe a word he says. So we're running another check on him. The works. But until and unless we can at least nail a record onto him, his word has to stand as good as yours."

"What about this Needle Nose and The Ox?" said Ballard.

"Give us last names," said Rubison. "You think those handles are unusual?" He chuckled. "I could name funnier. Half the hoods in the world have crazy aliases. They push screwy names on each other like a bunch of goddamn Indians. And there must be half a dozen right in this town they call Ox and maybe one or two Needle Nose. But they don't appear in the local mug book."

"In this town, no," said Ballard. "What about Chicago?"

"Way ahead of you," said Rubison. "We've got it on the wire with your description of 'em. Chicago'll get back to us soon enough. And maybe with pictures. Then you come down and have a look. If you can make them, that is, identify them, it'll put the show an the road."

"I'll tell you, one thing," said Kohler. "When you've got names like that, ninety-nine times out of a hundred, you've got criminals. And any time one of those out-of-state characters enters this county and he's been convicted of a felony, he's got five days to check in with the police department. The sixth day we can grab him and throw him in the pokey for failing to register."

"Great," said Ballard. "But before you can grab, you have to catch."

Kohler smiled, turning to Rubison. "Harry," he said, "whatta you think of this guy? A regular one-man police force, old style. Three muscle-happy pugs bust his face open and does he take it lying down? No! He's hardly out of the sheets and he shoves Beef Costigan around until he hollers Gould, then he plays cozy with this Maxine and suddenly he's back with news. We could use you, Ballard," His face grew stern. "But not your methods."

"I dunno," said Rubison, smiling. "Off the record, I kind of like his methods, too."

"What did you expect?" said Ballard. "What the hell would you do if three gorillas cut you to ribbons and you couldn't get the smallest satisfaction from the law?"

"I'd hunt those bastards down if it took a year," said Kohler. "And on my own time I'd do it the same way you did. But on duty I'd have to play it a lot cozier. You understand? Officially we don't sanction this rough stuff." He gave Rubison a wink.

"Hey!" Rubison said. "Did you know this guy was All-American out of Michigan?"

Kohler nodded solemnly. "Sure. He looks it, too."

"Michigan State," said Ballard. "And how did you know?"

"We make it our business to know a lot of things," said Kohler with hardly a smile.

Ballard was a little embarrassed and changed the subject abruptly. "So what about Gould?" he said. "Isn't he the one to rope first?"

Kohler shook his head. "Nope. Nothing on him at all. His whole operation is clean. In fact, they know him upstairs and the word is to go slow."

"You mean he's got a finger in the political pie!"

said Ballard angrily. "Is that it?"

"I didn't say that," answered Kohler. "The word is to go slow — but to go. There's a difference. I can't speak for Broward County and all of Dade, either. But if this particular department can smell a syndicate operation behind whatever cover, you can bet on all-out, full-scale effort. As far homicides, there are several unsolved on the books along with a rash of missing-person cases listed as possible homicides. If there's a tie-in, so much the better. But we need evidence, we need witnesses.

"Now, if you have to satisfy this grudge, and officially you have no right being mixed up in police work at all, then the best thing you can do is to get a real tender arm around this Maxine and bring her in ready to talk. Coddle her, give her a snow job, put the fear of God into her, but whatever you have to do, waltz her down here with the facts. Then we can crucify these birds without a comeback. I'm sorry, but for the time being, that's all we have to offer."

"Why can't you talk to Maxine? Maybe she'd listen to you."

"No," said Kohler. "She'll have to come to us. If she's in deep, we'd only scare her off. And maybe shake up trouble for her by showing our faces. When she's ready, she'll talk. That's your job, if you want it. And I sure as hell wouldn't. Not in your shoes. What's the girl's last name?"

"Bowman. That's the name she gave me, anyway."

"Maxine Bowman," he muttered and wrote it on a piece of paper. On another slip he wrote something and passed it to Ballard. "That's my name and two phone numbers. If you can't reach me here, call me at the one marked *Home.* Any time of the night, if you've got something worth getting me out of bed. But no fairy tales; facts you can substantiate, witnesses willing to sing loud and clear and on key. Okay?"

"Okay," said Ballard, pocketing the slip and going to the door.

"Good luck," said Kohler. "And listen, fellow, let me give you some advice, some good advice that I know goddamn well you're not gonna take. You get hold of that Maxine and get her fanny down here fast. But if you can't persuade her, then leave her alone and everyone else connected with this business. Let us handle it. You've got a lot of beef under that jacket, but you better use what's under here, the old noodle. Because, buddy, I've never yet seen enough brawn on a man to stop even a twenty-two-caliber slug in the right place. Know what I mean?"

"I know what you mean," said Ballard sincerely. "And thanks."

He closed the door behind him.

It was early afternoon now and he wanted nothing but sleep. The warm sun, the jog of car on highway as he drove home, relaxed tension and made him drowsy. He was tired of trouble and he tried to blank his mind. But sleepy or not, it wouldn't work. Dark clouds of thought drifted past for inspection.

Maxine had said they were planning a murder. That was absolutely all she would say. He had questioned her with smooth indirection but she kept repeating that it was late and she didn't want to talk about it. She had been on an emotional binge and when she sobered up, she was like the dunk who regrets all his acts the next morning. She withdrew into that cubicle of fear where she dwelt in lonely solitude, distant and uncommunicative.

Well, his personal can game had worked — up to a point. Now he would have to came up with another angle or wait until Maxine broke under her own pressures.

He had gone home with her just as dawn was break-ing. At least he followed her home. She had come is her own car.

He insisted that under the circumstances, she have an escort. He did want to see if she was being tailed or if her place was being watched. He also wanted to be able to back up his pretense of knowing where she lived.

The apartment house was located not more than two miles south of the Tropic Owl. It was a four-unit affair fashioned in the style of a colonial mansion. Of course, it was on the ocean and, of course, Maxine had the best layout in the building. She could afford it.

He was sure they were not followed and there did not appear to be anyone watching the place. But he went on up with her to her second-floor, beach-front apart-ment and looked around until she was satisfied no one had broken in while she was gone. He left her with a promise that he would stop by the Tropic Owl that night and chat with her between shows.

*H*e had slept until ten, barely three hours. After he had showered and dressed, he had called Lieutenant Kohler and made an appointment for 1 p.m. He didn't feel like cooking his own breakfast, so he drove to Fort Lauderdale and had French toast at the Colonel's Table in the Governors Club Hotel. From there, it was only a block to the Daily News where he went through the morgue of back issues.

There were no recent murders that seemed to have any possible connection with organized crime. There were, however, two notable disappearances. One had occurred about the time Ballard was beaten in the bar; it was the case of the high-ranking Miami judge, Wil-liam j. Hoffsteader, and his wife. Ballard went over this item, refreshing his memory.

Hoffsteader and his wife had gone to a dinner party in Miami. Police estimated that they must have arrived at their secluded Hillsboro Beach home around 11 p.m. They had no servants and were alone in the house. They were not missed until the following day when the judge did not make his customary appearance on the bench.

After a phone call which failed to get an answer, an officer was sent to the house. He found the front door closed but unlocked. He entered. Nothing had been disturbed. Beds were turned down and apparently had been slept in. There was a light burning in Mrs. Hoffsteader's room, but no evidence of a struggle. All else was in order. The judge's automobile was properly placed in the car port.

But at the water's edge, the officer found evidence that a small boat had been beached. And on the sand there was a blanket which was later proved to have come from Mrs. Hoffsteader's bed.

During that day and many to follow, the place swarmed with police. No prints were found and no tire tracks. There was not a single clue but the blanket and the impression made by a boat on the sand.

Authorities were forced to conclude that the Hoffsteaders were kidnapped over water. It was their guess that someone had rung the doorbell and the judge had come sleepily to answer. He was taken prisoner. And while he was being held, his wife, still in night clothes, was wrapped in a blanket and removed with him to a waiting launch. The blanket was dropped in the haste to be gone. It bore a small stain of blood. Footprints leading from the house had been eradicated.

It was further conceded that Mrs. Hoffsteader had become involved only because she had awakened and was thus a witness. Motive for the judge's kidnapping and probable murder was perhaps hidden somewhere is the records of his sentencing of numerous criminals. But when police were unable to pin the crime on any of these criminals, the case remained unsolved.

A more recent disappearance was that of another man and his wife, Mr. and Mrs. Paul Vulpiani, a wealthy couple who vanished from their home in Miami near Biscayne Boulevard. They had two servants but these did not live an the premises. A third occupant of the house was the Vulpianis' daughter Margaret, aged twenty-seven, who was visiting in Clearwater when her parents disappeared.

The Vulpianis had apparently been taken from their home sometime after they returned from a movie. In this case, there were blood smears on two of the wall surfaces, these made by the victims. There was no other conclusive evidence. Neither money nor possessions were missing. Another unsolved case.

Paul Vulpiani was a retired builder and, aside from the fact that he had said his business and had, come south from Chicago, Ballard could find no clue there, either. A countless number of people poured in from Chicago every day and it could be coincidence that Gould's operations were in Chicago. But at the right time, it would be worth investigating.

Leaving the Daily *News,* Ballard went next to the station and closeted himself with Ray Sawyer, his general manager. With the tourist traps coming down the home stretch for the richest part of the winter gravy, business was good. Many of the hotels and night clubs had more than doubled their advertising.

Ballard told Sawyer that he was counting on him to run the show for a short but indefinite period. Ray had been in the hospital to see Ballard and, at the time, had been told about the beating. Ballard said now that he

was close to finding the bastards who had clobbered him
— too close to give up. Ray nodded gravely, said he
understood and not to worry about the business. Aside
from the fact that he was a friend, he was getting a
percentage and he wasn't exactly loafing around. More
than satisfied with the way the operation was going,
Ballard left after Sawyer promised he would call if there
was an emergency.

The talk with Lieutenant Kohler and Sergeant Rubison had followed. He had gone to the interview with a
chip on his shoulder. The police were slow, full of red
tape and politics, stale policy and cumbersome routine.
They wouldn't do any more for him now than they had
in the past. But he wasn't such a damn fool as to carry
the weight of murder and lesser syndicate evil alone just
because of a personal need for justice and vengeance. It
wasn't worth the price of admission, the odds against
him were fantastic and, anyway, he wasn't going to make
a career of the whole goddamn thing. All he had started
out to do was bash a few heads, collect damages, and
maybe put three bastards behind bars where they could
think it over for a year or two. And now he was knee-deep
in what apparently was an empire of crime. It was like
going up a tree to catch a town cat who had scratched
you and finding in the dark cluster of branches a great
panther with bared fangs and muscles coiled for the
spring. So even if the police didn't break out the riot
guns and rush off into action, there was some sense in
telling the keepers of the crime zoo there was a panther
loose and letting them carry or fumble from there. It was
their zoo, not his; let *them* fill the cages. He was sure
they would fumble it, but he damn well wasn't even
going to try to recover. It was their ball from now on.

Surprisingly though, he had come away from the
talk with Kohler and Rubison feeling satisfied. They

hadn't done much of anything spectacular. But they were quietly working behind the scenes within the limits of reason and regulation and these two at least were, after all, quite human. He had the feeling that their restraint was official, not personal, and that when the chips were down and the word was Go, they would be guys you would be glad to have flanking you at the kickoff.

When he climbed into bed that afternoon and set the alarm for 9 p.m., he had some assurance of solid backing. Sleep stole upon him with the speed of winter darkness at sunset.

Chapter Eight

At ten o'clock that night, the supper-club tier of the Tropic Owl was bulging with customers. It looked as though there wouldn't be standing room in another half-hour.

"I'm glad you came, Gil," said Paula warmly, over the blare of music. "I hoped you would. And I saved the same table."

There was a softness and guilelessness in her face that he found charming. Unlike Maxine, no shadows of fear spoiled her features, no core of evil knowledge hardened her eyes.

She was not without her sensual side, but her sensuality was native, unstudied. She was sophisticated, even worldly, but her worldliness was not sordid. And now that he was certain that her involvement with Russ Gould was innocent, she became not only attractive but likable. Yet he was far too distracted to appreciate her.

"Thanks for saving a table," he said. "Sorry I had

to desert you last night, Paula. I'll make it up tonight. Okay?"

"You mean I have a ride home?"

"At least."

"You're an angel. But it's a long wait." She smiled, was about to say something, then had to find a table for a chubby man and his chubbier wife. She came back.

"You were saying?"

"I was about to say that maybe Maxine would entertain you until the last show — if she-ever gets here."

"She's late?"

"Very. They've been trying to reach her without any luck at all. She's probably on the way right now."

"Probably," said Ballard. But he was worried.

"You'd better grab that table," said Paula.

"Okay," he said. "You stay here and come over when you're not so busy." He gave bet arm a squeeze and left her.

The floor show was nearly half an hour late beginning. And when it did get underway, there were Playmates, but no Maxine. The band leader announced that she had been delayed unavoidably but would be on tap for the second show.

The Playmates did their best, but without Maxine, the act went pretty dead and was received with only mild applause.

Before it was over, Ballard had made an excuse to Paula and was racing to Maxine's apartment.

Her car was there in the parking lot of the building. He climbed the stairs two at a time, tried the door and found it open. He went in with Beef Costigan's .32 revolver in his hand.

The place was dark. He felt far a light switch and he flicked it on. The living room seemed in good order. Then he noticed that one of the heavy window drapes hung awry. He examined it. Half a dozen or so hooks that held it to the traverse rod had been zipped out, as though someone had clung to the drape and the pull had almost torn it down.

He went through the other rooms carefully. There was no disorder, but Maxine was gone. Her show costume hung with a rack full of dresses in her bedroom closet. A double bed with a pink coverlet had been neatly made.

He was leaving the room when he observed the black and white stuffed panda. He had noticed it an her bureau that warning and had mentioned it. She said it was a memento someone had given her and she kept it around because she thought it was cute.

There was something different about the big fuzzy panda. He picked it up and examined it. The difference was in the nose. Two-thirds of a sewing needle protruded from the black center of it, angling downward. He was positive the needle had not been there before because at the time he hoed been amused enough to look at the toy carefully. Furthermore, the needle stuck in the nose didn't make sense with a pincushion sitting right nest to the panda.

On the other hand, if Maxine thought he might have reason to come looking for her, the needle made a lot of sense. She could have had just time enough to jab it into the nose, sending a message which might be translated "Needle Nose was here and that's why I'm gone . . ." It could be coincidence, but Ballard didn't think so. Probably Needle Nose had been there. And maybe The Ox and Gould also. They might have set the Chicago dodge up as an alibi.

He began to look around again, this time more carefully. He didn't find anything until he had closed the front door behind him and flashed his light on the terrazzo floor just outside. There was it spot of blood the size of a half-dollar and next to it a smaller one. There were others at intervals, receding toward the stairs and then vanishing altogether.

A panda toy with a needle in its nose, a wrenched drape, Maxine's car in the lot and spots of blood — enough to guess that Maxine had taken an unexpected trip. And that the trip was one-way, absolute, final. Unless she could be found and found in a hurry! Even then . . .

*B*ack at the Tropic Owl they were turning people away and Paula said, "Sorry, Gil, but I couldn't hold your table. It's a madhouse."

"Never mind," he said. "When Maxine doesn't show for f the second go-round, you may have some seats."

Her face clouded. "You don't think she'll make it?"

"I don't think she'll make it."

"Gil! Do you know something I don't?"

"Maybe."

"Listen," she said quickly. "You ought to talk with Russ. He just phoned me from Chicago and he's worried."

"Gould just phoned!"

"Yes."

"Are you sure he was calling from Chicago?"

"Yes. There's something he wants me to decide and he gave me a number where I could reach him there."

"Did you mention me?"

"No, Gil, I'm sorry. There was so much excitement about Maxine and everything . . ."

"It doesn't matter. Is this a private number he gave you?"

"No. The Palmer House. He's been staying there for the last few days."

"I see." But he didn't see at all. Of course, Could might have sent his boys to take care of Maxine. Or it could have happened hours ago. There were fast planes . . .

"Paula," he said, "I've got to talk to you. Alone."

"Really, Gil, I can't. Not now."

"It's important. Very."

She must have seen the tension in his face. Without a word she went away. When she came back, she said, "The maitre d' will handle it for a while. This way."

He followed her to a small office beside the checkroom. She switched on the light. There was a tiny desk and two straight-backed chairs. Cases of liquor and mix stood against the walls. She closed the door and locked it. They sat down. He leaned toward her.

"Paula," he said, "I like you — one hell of a lot in a short time. What's more, I'm going to take the longest chance of my life and trust you."

"I'm flattered, Gil. But I don't understand."

He leaned closet. "Do you see these scars around the mouth, the eyes, up here an the temple?"

"Yes. I saw them before and I was curious, but I didn't want to . . ."

"I'll tell you where I got those scars, Paula. Russ Could and two of his goons, Needle Nose and The Ox, gave them to me. More than a month ago they sapped me in a bar and while one held me, the other two beat my face to ribbons with brass knuckles. Until day before yesterday I was in the hospital getting glued together. They beat me because I played the same juke record once too often and they were annoyed. But until that night I had never heard of Russell Gould or anyone connected with him. So try to imagine what they would do if they were just a little more than annoyed, Paula."

He had been watching her intently as he spoke. Her astonishment was genuine. Her mouth hung open. She was incredulous.

"I can't believe it," she gasped.

"I expected that," he said. "So I'll give you a synopsis of the whole dirty mess. It goes a lot deeper than that beating, deeper than my need to step on Gould until he breaks apart."

Quickly he ran down the details for her.

"So you see," he wound up, "that toothy smile of Gould's is hiding a lot of garbage."

"And you think they got Maxine?" she said with hushed voice, her face white.

He shrugged. "It seems obvious to me."

"Have you called the police?"

"Not about this. Not yet. And with what? A torn drape and a few blood spats that could be from a nose bleed? With those boys you practically have to deliver a corpse."

The line of her jaw hardened. "I never had any idea," she said. "I was innocent as the day I was born. Poor Max. Is there anything I can do?"

"Good girl! There may be a lot you can do. What did Could say on the phone? Did you tell him about Maxine?"

"Yes. It's disgusting. He sounded so shocked. But he said not to worry, that he knew her well and she was a secret drinker and that when slue got drunk, sometimes she just wandered off somewhere on a kind of lost weekend. Then she would come back and be sorry and not remember a thing about it. He said he had had to fire her a couple of times. But she had talent and he always got soft — imagine! — got soft and hired her back. He said this time she was through and he was sending a replacement."

He nodded. "That's about the kind of story I expected. But this is one lost weekend slue may not come out of."

"I don't get it," she said. "If Russ is in Chicago . . ."

"A short hop by plane. Maybe he was setting up an alibi. What was this decision he wanted you to make?"

"Well, he said he was the controlling partner in an organization that had built a fabulous new hotel on the outskirts of Golden Beach. It's the last word, with a private club on the top floor and . . ."

"The Oasis?"

"Yes. I've seen it going up fast. You look and there's a foundation. Then you look again and there's a building."

"It's the latest and the biggest," said Ballard. "I suppose he wanted you over there."

"Right. In the club part. To help get things organized and then stay on if I like it. He told me to think about it and call him back in an hour." She looked at her watch. "That would be in five minutes."

"Tell him you'll go."

"What!"

"Tell him you'll do it. According to Maxine, he's overboard for you. I think if you dropped a few hints about having a slightly shady background and played up to him, you could get some information. Somehow we've got to find out where they took Maxine. And fast!"

"I'd be scared to death."

"Well, it's a small help, but I'll be in touch all the time. Will you do it?"

"If it will help Maxine, yes. I haven't any choice."

"Good. Where can you phone?"

"Downstairs."

"Then go call him. But first, tell me if there's any

place you can think of where they might be holding Maxine.''

She shook her head. "There's this night club and there's the house. That's about as much as I know.''

"What about the boat yard?''

"It doesn't look like a place to hide anyone.''

"Does Russ own any kind of boat?''

"Yes, a yacht. He took me along with him once on a fishing party.''

"Where does he keep it?''

"I don't know where he usually keeps it. But that day it was docked in front of someone's house on a canal off the Intracoastal, between Dania and Hollywood. The house was closed. He said it belonged to a Chicago friend of his who let him use the dock, for convenience.''

"Do you think you can tell me how to get there?''

"I can try.''

He produced a piece of paper and a pen. "Draw me a map with landmarks.''

She made a quick sketch, explaining her markings. "Okay," he said. "This will do it. Now, make your call. I'll be back by closing to take you home. Look for me outside.''

She stood up and, at the door, he held her and kissed her. She was trembling. "I'm not very brave," she said. "I'm just plain scared.''

"So's Maxine," he said. "You'll do fine. I'm counting on you.''

Chapter Nine

*F*ollowing Paula's map, Ballard went south from Dania on Route A1A a little better than a mile. Here he crossed a bridge over the Intracoastal and drove west until he came to a series of canals that emptied into the Coastal. At the west tip of one of these branches, he found the house, a pick sandstone tri-level peering over a stone wall with an iron-grille gate.

The gate was locked and the house was dark, hurricane shutters sealing the windows. The wall enclosed a good deal of property, the nearest house being several hundred yards removed.

By standing atop the rear deck of the Pontiac, Ballard could reach up and get enough grip to hoist himself over the wall, thumping to the ground on the other side.

Hearing nothing but the wind-stir of palm fronds, he advanced through trees and shrubs to the water side of the house. Here there was a long spill of dock between pilings set in the canal bed. And taking up all but the entire length of it, an immense cruiser. A narrow gangway rose from the dock amidships and ran aboard. A single dim light came from a lower porthole.

Inspecting the house itself, Ballard noticed that, while the canal side was also shuttered, one of these had been partly raised and from beneath it came a small splay of light. Moving toward this light, he came to a driveway containing the shadowy outlines of a trio of expensive-looking cars. Two were Cadillacs, the third he couldn't make out.

Feeling uncomfortably committed for the sake of Maxine, Ballard advanced, kneeling beneath the shuttered window, squeezing in the small space and rising enough to see.

It was a living room, hazy with smoke. Almost a dozen men sat in a semicircular arrangement of chairs before a great fieldstone fireplace. They smoked, gulped from highball glasses and listened to the man who leaned against the mantel of the fireplace.

This man was Russell Gould!

It might have been the meeting of a group of businessmen. All were neatly, almost too neatly, attired in plain suits of gray, brown or charcoal, two or three wearing subdued sport coats and slacks. All had more or less the look of prosperity and the egocentric expression of command. But here the likeness to business executives ended. For, in the faces, some of them swarthy under dark, oiled hair, there was another similarity: hardness, smug greed and cruelty. And in the eyes, the bright shrewdness of the flat deadness of too much tolerance for, and too much acquaintance with, evil.

Not businessmen, thought Ballard, henchmen. A meeting of the top moguls of the Syndicate.

Gould, dressed in what looked like a dark gray shantung, beautifully tailored, was perhaps the one person in the room who seemed out of character. He looked, with his olive-smooth features, wavy black hair, flashing teeth, like some Latin movie star, a charming Montalban expanding in his role. Now his smile dazzled the room with persuasiveness, now his bushy brows were knit together with stern intensity over eyes sparkling with purpose. And now he leaned forward and drove home a point with fist on palm.

It was a pantomime, for the window was closed and only a murmur of sound reached Ballard.

Needle Nose was not to be seen. But lounging against a dosed door at one end of the room was the giant, glassy-eyed Ox.

Ballard stooped and backed away. Softly he padded his approach to the yacht, softly mounted the gangway and stepped aboard.

Finding the wheelhouse locked, he circled astern in the darkness, saw light through the glass of the after-cabin door, slid it gently back and stepped onto the enclosed deck. Crouching by a companionway, he peered below where light filtered down a passageway of closed stateroom doors.

A man sat by the door of one of the cabins in a deck chair. Across his lap, finger under trigger guard, he rested a submachine gun. There was about him a droopy watchfulness. He held the weapon with both hands while a cigarette dangled from his lips and smoke eddied from a sharp, slightly, curving nose.

Needle Nose.

Ballard could guess what was behind the door. But he did not think in his present position he was going to be able to take the gun away or even come close. And he knew he was not going to be foolhardy enough to try. Instead, he crept out and around on deck, looking for another entry. He could find none without the risk of breaking glass.

He was about to step ashore and peer into portholes when there was the faint tread of steps on the gangway. He stood frozen in place. There was not time to move. The big shadow was already upon him. He couldn't see the man's face but knew it was The Ox.

He struck mightily and the blow crashed against cheekbone. Ox grunted, fell backward, caught the edge of rail in time, plunged forward again to catch a fist in the windpipe. But his momentum carried him on to pin Ballard against the cabin while his big hands came up to circle Ballard's throat.

Though he was slowly being choked into oblivion, Ballard had only a distant sensation of pain. The bitter taste of another night in which there was violence with Ox holding him powerless, twisted inside him. And now his big fists went to work, ramming, crushing, beating upon The Ox's belly, chin, nose, eye socket and brow. And his knee shoved upward into the groin.

The Ox released him and doubled, backed away, dripping blood to the deck. A bad mistake. Ballard's fist came up from far below and splintered his jaw.

As The Ox fell mightily to the deck, there was the quick beat of ascending steps. Needle Nose was coming up the companionway. Ballard could picture him with the submachine gun carried at part and ready. Much more sound in a hush so deep and soon a dozen men might come running, perhaps clutching at shoulder holsters.

Ballard leaped over The Ox and ran nimbly on the balls of his feet, forward around the deck to the water side, then aft. While Needle Nose could be heard busy with The Ox, he noiselessly opened the door to the after-cabin and slid below.

The key was in the lock. He turned it and entered

darkness, ready to untie Maxine and carry her to safety. But in the gloom there were only sealed boxes, empty bunks. The boxes must contain interesting secrets, but they would have to wait. There vas a growing sound of voice and movement on deck.

Ballard went back swiftly as he came, trying doors along the way, finding them locked. From the bow he peered around the superstructure. The Ox was on his knees, trying to get up. Needle Nose was lighting the darkness with a flash, the gun sweeping with the cone of light.

"Who did it?" said Needle Nose, his voice hungry with the need of action.

"Dunno," said The Ox, wobbling to his feet. His voice had a slushy sound and blood poured from a corner of his mouth. Under the light his nose was bruised and canted, there was a cut under his eye, a welt on his temple, a livid swelling on his jaw.

One down and two to go, thought Ballard.

"Come on, come an!" said Needle Nose. "Who creamed you?"

The Ox shook his head to clear it. "Tole ya I dunno. Big bastard. Came to tell ya they're comin' aboard, coupla minutes. Sonofabitch waiting on deck. I catch 'im, I'll kill 'im!"

"Couldn't of been one of oar boys," said Needle Nose. "One of them had a grudge, he'd finish you."

"All inside, anyway," said The Ox.

"Come on!" said Needle Nose. "Must be still on the grounds."

They went down the gangplank and the light could be seen bobbing away into the outer darkness toward the wall.

Ballard leaped off in two bounds, ran to a comer of the house, fell prone behind a thick growth of shrubs and waited. Again Costigan's revolver was in his hand.

In a moment Needle Nose's flash approached, sprayed within a foot of his position and went on. The Ox and Needle Nose now stood by the gangway, waiting. They were rewarded in less than a minute when there was the sound of a door closing and shadows drifted over the back lawn to their position. It looked like the entire assembly.

There was some low, inaudible conversation, an occasional sharp oath. Then several of the men went aboard while others remained ashore. What followed was the heaving of boxes hand-to-hand down the gangway and the passage of the boxes to others who carried them to the cars and promptly drove off with an angry splat and crunch of gravel.

At this point, Ballard was happy that he had thought to conceal his car around a far bend of the wall. And now as he watched, the flash winked on and Gould, Needle Nose, The Ox and another climbed aboard. There was the whine of starter; the throaty purr of engines. Someone came back down to cast off ropes, reboarded and helped hoist the gangplank. Running lights winked on arid the yacht moved off, gathering speed.

Ballard was alone.

At least that was his hope as he found the open and forgotten storm shutter, broke a window with a brick wrapped in the fold of his jacket and entered behind his pencil flash and gun.

It was a big house and the search of it without risking central light was an ordeal of strange objects, monstrous shadows and unknown mysteries behind doors. But, in the end, he found he was right. He was all too alone. Not a shred of clothing or any other belonging in drawer or closet. It was a house of furniture.

From the beginning, Maxine must have been

aboard the yacht, in one of many locked cabins. Perhaps eau now the yacht was putting out to sea for her destruction. And that yacht contained an arsenal of defense.

Yet, could he prove that she was on board? I swear it, Lieutenant Kohler. I feel it, I know it! And I saw the gun and the boxes. And the hoods in meeting.

Not enough, Ballard, shaking his head gravely. Bring me evidence! Bring me Maxine Bowman . . .

Chapter Ten

*T*he Tropic Owl was all but dark. Paula came out and down the steps in nervous haste, her features pulled tight with worry.

Ballard opened the car door and slue said, "Any mews, Gil? Anything at all?"

She climbed in and Ballard drove off. "Nothing," he said. "Nothing but a guess. You called Chicago — the Palmer House?"

"Yes."

"Of course Gould wasn't there."

"You're wrong, Gil. He was there, all right."

"What!"

"I talked with him."

He turned quickly to look at her. Either she was lying or — "Let me get this straight. You called the Palmer House in Chicago, you asked for Russell Gould, they rang his room and he answered. That right?"

"Almost. But not quite. I called and they rang his room and another man answered. He said just a moment and then he came back and told me that Russ must have stepped out for a minute, probably went down to the bar for a drink. He got my name, said he'd locate Russ and have him call me right back."

Ballard was beginning to understand. "And did he call right back?"

"Yes. In about ten minutes. He wasn't at the bar. He had been visiting with some people in another room."

"He wasn't in Chicago at all," said Ballard. "He was right here in town. I saw him a couple of hours ago. What must have happened was this: he was registered, he did have a room, but he had someone else sweating out the phone. This guy called Gould here and Gould called you. Simple. But what makes it damn complicated and very bad, is that he needed an alibi. And if someone goes to that much trouble to establish an alibi — well, think it over."

"You actually saw Russ!"

"Like Cinemascope."

He told her the events of the night, Paula making worried sounds throughout.

"From the way you describe it," she said finally, "it doesn't sound like the same yacht I was on. Much bigger, I would think. Did you get the name of it?"

"It was too dark and I was too busy. But I'd recognize it."

"Are you going to hunt for it?"

"Of course. But there are hundreds of waterways and hundreds of yachts. I wouldn't be surprised if there were more in this area than any place in the world."

"But you, think Max is onboard?"

"Is — or was." They were riding along the coast and he looked out to sea. "It's a big ocean out there."

"Oh, God. You think they . . ."

"I don't want to think. I have to know. But the sad truth is that they do have her. And I can't conceive of any logical reason why they would just hold her prisoner. Too risky and pointless. Alive and talkative, she's poison. And dead, she tells a mute but even dirtier story. So they would warn to dispose of her quickly. And an ocean is the world's most uncommunicative dispose-all.''

"How brutal it sounds."

"I'm sorry, Paula. But if you want to outguess criminals, you have to think in cold-blooded, practical terms. Underneath I'm, well . . . I'll tell you this — I've got a reasonable amount of guts, maybe more than average because I'm used to force and physical punishment and objectively, at least, I understand something about these hoods and their methods. But I'm not too dumb to be afraid of a gun when it's pointed in my direction by someone who means to use it. And if it wasn't for Maxine I'd be happy to write my beating off the books and try to forget it ever happened. Hell, crime will destroy itself if you give it enough time. Most gangsters don't die in electric chairs or gas chambers but from their own bullets. Yet, I can't just say Maxine is probably dead and let's forget it.''

"Then you don't think it's hopeless?''

"I think there's about one chance in a hundred. And I have to gamble on it.''

He was watching the rearview wow. But behind him, the road was empty of traffic.

"I'll do anything in the world I can to help," she said. "But I'm worried about you, Gil. You plunge right into things so wholeheartedly where the average person would be winging around waiting for the police.''

"Sometimes that's a long wait — though it isn't always their fault.''

"How do you know so much about crime and police work?''

"It used to fascinate me. In a negative sort of way, it still does. Because there's nothing penny-ante about this whole operation. It's a clever network, smooth, efficient, merciless."

"You still haven't answered my question."

"How do I know anything about crime? As I said, it used to fascinate me. I used to ride with a homicide prowl car. I wanted to be a detective. I studied furiously and I saw the whole business firsthand."

"But you never became a detective. Why?"

"It wasn't as exciting as I thought it was. Mostly plodding routine. And the characters they chased down most of the time weren't like Gould. They were boobs that anyone with common sense and an ounce of know-how could figure out. No challenge. Not to mention the pay. And I don't like violence just for its own sake. The only part that really interested me was the solving of a difficult puzzle."

He swung across the road and pulled up by a stretch of beach beyond which the ocean was just a ruffled etching inked against the night.

"Anything wrong?" said Paula.

"No, nothing." He doused the lights. "But we're almost at Gould's and there are still things I have to know and discuss."

"You're not coming in? Russ certainly won't be there."

"No, but his bop Carl has eyes and ears all over the place. I'm surprised he hasn't been tailing us tonight. And you can't tell who else might be nosing around there."

"That's true. It wouldn't be wise."

He leaned back against the door, lighted a pair of cigarettes, gave her one. "Now," he said. "What arrangement did you make with Gould?"

"According to his lying story, he's supposed to be flying down tomorrow night — tonight, I mean — and going right to The Oasis. That will be the first night of the hotel's operation. It actually opens at noon today with a lot of flag-waving. But strangely, he isn't even going to be there. He seems much more interested in this private club on the top floor. It has its own dining room, bars, entertainment and what not. The rooms on the two floors below it are for club members only. It's a regular hotel within a hotel, according to him."

"Mmmm. If that's his main interest, it must have some shady implications. What's the name of the club?"

"It's called the Topsiders Club."

"Great. What I want to knows is, what goes on below deck?"

"I think I can tell you one thing."

"What?"

"He asked me if I objected to a little wheeling and dealing. I said, 'What do you mean?' And he said, 'Gambling.'"

"Wow! Now there's one I don't get at all. Gambling used to be nearly wide open around here. But they put the lid on and what there is of it is so far under wraps you'd have a tough time finding a back-room dice game. On the other hand, there was a recent political shake-up and there are some new faces in the higher echelons of the police departments. There's got to be a feedline somewhere. Anyway, what did you tell him?"

"I told him I didn't object at all, that I loved gambling. I said that as a matter of fact I used to work in a New York night club that had gambling before it closed down. Fortunately he didn't ask me which one. But I had a name ready on the tip of my tongue, a place I knew really did have gambling at one time."

"So how did that impress him?"

"I got the feeling that he was terrifically pleased and trying to conceal it. He said, kind of jokingly, 'Paula, I thought you were a little girl scout who was completely uneducated in any of the forms of vice.'

"And I said, 'Oh, you'd be surprised, Russ. Don't let that innocent look fool you.' He was chuckling all over the place and eating right out of my hand."

Ballard was thoughtful. "Do you mind if I ask a personal question, Paula?"

"I won't know until you ask me."

"I imagine Russ has had the opportunity. Has he ever tried to make you?"

"Are you kidding!"

"No," he said a little too solemnly. "I'm perfectly serious."

"He tries all the time — very smoothly, that is. Subtle. But it's practically an obsession with him. I don't think he's ever had anyone refuse him before and it drives him crazy."

"Thanks. That answers my question."

"Not altogether. I'll be perfectly honest with you, Gil. Before I knew about him I was attracted to him. He has a lot of magnetism. There were a couple of close calls. I mean, you know, necking getting almost out of hand. But I never gave in to him. And now I absolutely loathe him."

"You didn't have to tell me that. But thanks. It would have been difficult for me to believe Gould would hang around any girl if there wasn't at least hope. And I guess there is a certain sadistic charm about him."

"I didn't know it was sadistic at the time."

"Of course not. And now just go ahead and give him all kinds of hope. Not rope — hope."

She laughed. "Don't worry."

"I'll take care of the rope," he said. "Right around

his neck. When do you meet him and where?"

"Nine o'clock at the Topsiders. He said things wouldn't really get underway until ten and he could show me around. He's already got someone to take my place at the Tropic Owl and the replacement for Maxine starts tonight."

"My God. The bastard! What job has he got for you?"

"He's going to explain it."

"Obviously he wants to be real chummy with you but he can't until he works you into the operation and he can trust you. So play it for all it's worth. Pump hell out of him but for God's sake don't be obvious. And find out anything you can about that yacht. You can ask him when he's going to take you for another cruise, something like that. Keep your eyes open; snoop around but don't get caught. Unfortunately, we've got practically anything but time. So you'll have to accomplish wonders the first night. You've got one big ace and that's sex appeal. You'll have to keep dealing it and pulling it back again damn cleverly, like, 'We're on the way, but let's not hurry it, Russ dear.' And, baby, I don't envy you."

"I can handle him, Gil. A woman knows those things."

"Right. Now, do you think you can get me up there for a quick look around?"

"I could try, but it would be terribly dangerous. Wouldn't he recognize you?"

"He might. And then again the chances are he wouldn't. The bar was dark and it was a mere incident in his life, of no real importance to him. He was just beating an anonymous face; almost like satisfying the urge to eat raw steak with him. Long forgotten. But he's not going to be on the floor every, minute. He'll have an office. Get me up there when he's away and then try to keep him busy. I know you can think of one or two ways. Meantime, I'll be down in the lobby, using the name Gillman to be on the safe side, old Charlie Gillman. You have me paged and tip me to come up. Okay?''

"What time?''

"I'll wait there from ten on.''

"Somehow I'll do it, Gil. I'll just have to.''

"You're a brave girl, Paula. And I wish I could tell you how much I hate to use you as bait. You, of all people.''

She tossed her cigarette out the window. "Don't tell me, Gil, show me. Show me how much it matters.'' She leaned toward him. "Because if I'm going to be any good with Russ, I'll need to know. Otherwise, I'll be so scared I'll fall apart.''

"I'll show you, ail right,'' he said softly, pulling her against him.

And he did.

It was a long time before he drove her home.

Chapter Eleven

‘Sure, Lieutenant,'' said Ballard in the morning as he looked at the pictures, ‘'this is The Ox and this is Needle Nose. No doubt about it at all.''

Lieutenant Kohler took the pictures back from Ballard, tossed them on his desk. ‘'Ox Kowalski and Needle Nose Tabrino,'' he said. ‘'Chicago hoods. Armed robbery, assault with a deadly weapon, possession of stolen goods, suspicion of murder; you name it, they've done it. They used to commute between Chicago and Joliet. Then they dropped out of sight. Nothing on them in years. The dope came in this morning.''

‘'So?'' said Ballard. ‘'I gave you the story: a machine gun, boxes of God-knows-what — and Maxine Bowman missing. You going to pick them up?''

‘'We'll pick 'em up, all right,'' said Kohler. ‘'If we can find 'em. But that's no guarantee we can hold 'em.''

‘'What about Gould?''

Kohler smiled. ‘'Real name, not Gould, but Giuliano. Not Russell, but Salvatore. Salvatore Giuliano. Three arrests a long time ago, no convictions. Clean as new snow ever since.''

"And what are you going to do about him?''

Kohler shook his head. "Nothing.''

"Nothing?''

"Nothing," said Kohler flatly. "We have nothing on him and the word is strictly hands off.''

"Christ!" said Ballard. "Do I have to go upstairs?''

"That's where the word came from," said Kohler disgustedly. "This stuff about your friend Giuliano, I got on my own. It could cost me.''

"You mean, the fix is in," said Ballard.

Kohler scowled, leaned forward. "I'd advise you to keep a tight lip on that kind of talk," he said. "You could get into trouble.''

"Crap!" Ballard said. "I give up.''

"Listen," said Kohler confidentially, "I know how you feel. I'm in your alley. I'm so goddamn mad myself, I'm about to blow a gasket. But we got a new broom upstairs a little while ago. And from all the talk, I thought the broom was gonna sweep clean. Then I find out the goddamn handle is broken and all the bristles fell out. Know what I mean?''

"So where does that leave us? Is there anyone at the top you can trust?''

"Sure. The DA, Barry Saunders. You bring me some evidence of a crime that will stand up, and I'll take it to Saunders myself. Then we'll see some heads roll — and I don't mean just The Ox, Needle Nose, and Salvatore, either.''

"Tell me something, Lieutenant, do you believe this staff I've been telling you about a syndicate meeting with Gould presiding, Maxine missing from her apartment and the rest of it?''

"Sure, I believe it. You haven't brought me Proof One, but I believe you."

"Then why in God's name don't you take it on yourself to round up some, boys and go after these bastards? You carry enough brass to shout some orders."

"I'll tell you why," said Kohler, getting up from his desk, crossing to a window, turning, coming back and sitting down again before he spoke. "Because it took one hell of a lot of years to put me in this seat. And I don't intend to lose it on a mere hunch that I can nail Giuliano with something that won't backfire me right out an my ass. Until I have evidence in writing, or I can catch someone in the act, or I can find someone who talks and points a finger, I can't afford to chance it when the order is don't touch, even with gloves."

"Okay," said Ballard. "So I'll give you evidence. Will gambling do?"

"Gould?"

"Yes."

Kohler smiled. "You mean the Topsiders Club?"

"Exactly."

"That's not gambling," said Kohler. "There's not going to be an exchange of money — just games for the private amusement of club members with a free prize to the biggest winner at the end of the year. Gould checked in on the legality of it long ago."

"So that's his story. Do you believe that crap?"

"No, not for a minute. There's got to be an angle but I don't think we're gonna find it. Some people won't even be trying. And if we do find it, I think it's gonna be a tough one to prove. But I'll guarantee you I'll have a man or two checking it out."

"Okay, Lieutenant," said Ballard. "I won't bother you again."

"On the contrary," said Kohler. "Any time you've

got something you can substantiate, I'm ready to grab my coat and run.''

"Never mind your coat," said Ballard. "Just grab your gun. So long, Lieutenant.''

Chapter Twelve

"Mr. Gilman, paging Mr. Charles Gilman! Call-for-Mr.-Gill-man!"

Gil Ballard looked at his watch. Ten after eleven. He had been wasting in the plush lobby of The Oasis an hour and ten minutes.

He followed the boy to the home phone, gave him a coin and picked up the receiver. "Gillman speaking."

"At any other time, I'd think that was funny," said Paula. "Sorry to keep you waiting, Gil. It's been hectic."

"I imagine. Can you talk freely?"

"Yes. I'm in a phone booth up here."

"Can you get me into the club?"

"You'll have to have a membership card wherever you, go. Russ had some tetras on his desk. I stole one and filled in your name. I mean Gillman."

"Old Charlie?"

"Old Charlie. And listen, this isn't funny. I'm a wreck. Ross has been breathing down my neck like a blowtorch. All I did was act a little willing and now the only escape is the powder room.''

"Just as long as you keep him running without catching. Did you ply any information?"

"About the gambling? It's a big joke. Signs all over the place shouting that gambling is illegal and this is purely for fun. You won't see a nickel cash. Just chips which are turned in, as credit toward a prize for the biggest winner. But the winnings are figured m dollars and the chips have fake money values from a dollar to a hundred. I asked Russ if the games were as innocent as they looked, and he just smiled and said, 'You'll learn, honey, soon enough.'''

"Anything about the yacht?"

"There are pictures of yachts in his office, one very big one. I asked him about it and he said, 'Oh, that belongs to a friend of mine from Chicago.' And then he got on the phone and I didn't have a chance to follow up. But I will. And it may not be easy. Because in spite of the fact that he's in hot pursuit, something's bothering him. He's worried."

"That boy's worries have only begun. Listen, can you remember what this yacht looked like?"

"It was painted a very dark color and it had one of those smoke things —"

"A stack?"

"Yes. And it had a lifeboat, too."

"Where was the lifeboat located?"

"I remember because it seemed like an odd place — at the stern."

"That's the one! You're on the beam. Did you notice the name?"

"Yes. *Sea Jet.*"

"Fine. We know what to look for. See if you can find out *where*. You're going good, Paula baby. Just be careful. Now, how do I get in?''

"Come up to Fifteen. There's a private elevator that goes from there to the next three floors. A guard will be at the elevator door checking membership cards. Eventually he's supposed to recognize every member. But tonight he's lucky if he knows ten. I'll come down, meet you on Fifteen, give you the card and go up with you in case he's suspicious. He knows who I am.''

"Does everyone have to have a card? How about guests?''

"There are no guests, only members, their wives, and a few single girls and men. They all have been checked practically from the time they were born, and they all have cards.''

"Sounds damn exclusive. Enough to make me mighty curious. Where's Gould at the moment?''

"He's in the office talking to the manager of the night club and entertainment end of the setup, a Mr. Pasquali. I'm supposed to work for Mr. Pasquali, but tonight I'm just doing a run-through and mostly playing patsy with Russ. He has a private bar and lounge adjoining the office and, as soon as I get back, we're going there for a drink. I don't care for that at all, but I'll keep him busy.''

"You're the greatest, sweetheart. Start down and I'll meet you on Fifteen. And listen, I'll be in the gaming room of whatever they call it here, most of the time. If you find out anything important, sneak in and give me a nod. Then I'll came back down to the lobby and you can phone me. It's safer. Okay?''

"Okay, Gil. Meet you in a couple of minutes.''

"Right.''

He hung up.

*P*aula was in the corridor on Fifteen. She wore a rose-colored, low-necked silk dress that performed beautifully around tight curves and still managed charm and good taste.

Her smile was worried and Ballard was suddenly filled with compassion for her. And just as suddenly he needed her and knew that she belonged and that the emptiness of Julie's loss could be filled.

"Paula, honey," he said. "I want you out of this. Give me the card, then you go home to our own apartment and wait for me. I can handle it."

"No, Gil. You're sweet, but no. I'm making progress. I've got to find out about that yacht and I'm not in the least danger from Russ."

"That's what Maxine thought, too."

"Tomorrow we'll talk about it. I've got to get back. All right?"

"Paula, I can't be objective about you any more. It's gone way past that. You understand?"

"I know," she said. "I had the feeling way before you did."

"That's because the pace is so fast, there hasn't been time for me to feel anything," he said. Lighting a cigarette, he glanced dawn the hall to where the uniformed guard was checking a club member into the elevator.

Paula squeezed his hand. "Come on," she said. "The pace hasn't changed yet. Let's not be conspicuous. Here's the card I fixed up for you. Now you're a member in very bad standing."

He glanced at the card. It had a number. His was 337. He dropped it into his pocket and together they walked to the elevator.

"Miss Schaeffer," said the guard with a small bow and a smile. "Evening, sir, going up."

"This is Mr. Gillman, Jimmy. One of our new members."

"How do you do, sir," said Jimmy. "See your card, please?"

Jimmy was of medium height with much muscle and the look of having put his manners on with his uniform only to find that both fit a little uncomfortably.

Ballard produced the card, Jimmy studied it, handed it back as the elevator arrived. "Know you next time, sir," he said.

Sure hope not, thought Ballard, giving the guard a wave and following Paula into the car. They ascended to the eighteenth and top floor.

"We'd better separate here," said Paula as they stepped from the elevator. "I go to the right and you go left for the gaming room."

He gave her a wink, said, "See you later," and they moved off in opposite directions.

Ballard walked over rich carpeting, peering into rooms off the corridor: a dim bar, a dining room, a night club with a large dance floor. All the rooms were splendid, if a little gaudy. All commanded extravagant views of city lights and water.

The gaming room was easily identifiable. It was called Cloud Seven and the activity could be seen through swinging glass doors beside which stood another guard in red jacket and black trousers. On the wall beside the doors hung a large sign ire red letters which read:

WARNING!

GAMBLING IS ILLEGAL IN THE STATE OF FLORIDA. THE GAMES IN THE ROOM ARE STRICTLY FOR THE AMUSEMENT AND FREE ENJOYMENT OF MEMBERS. THEY ARE NOT BE CONSTRUED AS GAMES OF CHANCE

AND, UNDER PENALTY OF EXPULSION, MEMBERS WILL
REFRAIN FROM ANY FORM OF WAGERING AMONG THEM-
SELVES WHICH INVOLVES MONEY OR REWARD.

IN ORDER TO PROMOTE INTEREST AND CREATE SOME
SMALL EXCITEMENT IN GAMES, A PRIZE WILL BE
AWARDED AT MIDNIGHT ON THE EVE OF EACH NEW YEAR.
THE PRIZE WILL BE A YEAR'S MEMBERSHIP FREE OF
DUES WITH THE MANAGEMENT PICKING UP THE TAB
FOR BAR, RESTAURANT, AND OTHER NORMAL EXPENSES
OF THE CLUB DURING THAT YEAR. MARRIED COUPLES
WILL BE CONSIDERED JOINT WINNERS WITH EQUAL
PRIVILEGES EXTENDED TO BOTH.

THERE WILL BE A SECOND PRIZE OF AN ALL-EX-
PENSES PAID, TEN-DAY CARIBBEAN CRUISE FOR TWO.

NATURALLY, PRIZES WILL GO TO THOSE WHO HAVE,
IN ONE YEAR, TURNED BACK TO THE MANAGEMENT AN
ACCUMULATION OF CHIPS BARING THE HIGHEST SIMU-
LATED MONETARY VALUE.

Ballard, wing studied the sign with some amazement, began to push through the doors when the guard
stopped him, politely but firmly asking for his membership card. Again he showed Paula's phony and was
passed inside.

It might have been one of the flashier gaming rooms
of Vegas or Reno, except that nowhere could there be
seen a coin or bill.

The room was elliptical and contained three crap
tables complete with croupiers rattling chips and dice,
a roulette wheel, and several tables of Twenty-one. Only
the slot machines were missing.

Lights above the tables glared and a pall of blue-
gray smoke ascended from the smoking equipment of
the better than a hundred expensively clad members
who filled the purified, moneyless gambling den, Cloud

Seven. If there was any visible sin, it was is the drinks being served by attractive waitresses who hovered near the tables for orders.

These orders were filled from semi-enclosed and softly lighted bars at two extremes of the room. They were not merely serving bars but contained stools, tables, and booths.

To one side of the entrance to the room, Ballard noted a large table containing an immense array of chips in "simulated" denominations of one, five, twenty-five, and a hundred dollars. Members would stop by this table for chips, paying nothing, of course, but showing their cards and having the amount of the chips recorded for the sake of the prize award.

There were two "simulated" cashiers at the table and Ballard spoke to the one who was presently idle, a small grab man in the red and black uniform of the club.

"Mind telling ms how this works?" he said. "I heard the details but I've forgotten."

"Certainly," said the man with a faint look of amusement "It's very simple. Here I have an alphabetical list of all the members. I find your name and in the red column, I place the amount of chips you have taken. At the end of your play, I place in the black column a figure representing the total in chip value you return. At the conclusion of the year, these are balanced against each other and then against the score of the other members. The largest winners take the prizes. Simple?"

"Oh, very," said Ballard.

"Would you like to play, sir?"

"No, thanks. Not just now. I'll watch a while."

"Very well, sir."

Ballard moved off, wondering just what would have happened had he shown his card and the man couldn't find his name on the membership list.

Walking casually from table to tabs, Ballard found himself more interested in the faces a£ the people than in the play. The faces told him something that was not evident in the innocuous-seeming mechanics of the games. For though the games were supposedly without risk of money, the faces of the players were often tense and strained, disproportionately excited or fearful. Why the tension and fear if you could never lose or win more than a free prize?

Ballard concluded that the gambling must be real and that the factors which made it real were hidden somehow in the bookkeeping. Since all but outsiders must be aware of the method it should not be difficult to learn the truth as he had so often before, by pretending to know it.

Of one thing Ballard was certain. The place was attracting some damn good-looking females. He had seen a number scattered about the room at various tables. In fact, there was an outstanding redhead at the crap table he was just now passing and he paused to stand beside her and watch her bets.

She was a girl in her twenties, long-haired with a pert little cameo of a face boasting an intriguing mouth which piled a lot with flashing displays of fine teeth. She wore a pale green gown decked from shoulder to bosom with a transparent black material. And though her structure was rather delicate and small-boned, her breasts were surprisingly large and also teasingly visible beneath the flimsy black gauze.

Although she would be a marvel of sex appeal at fifty feet, let alone two, Ballard observed that there was nothing cheap in her costume or manner. In fact, there was a certain aristocratic tilt to her fine head with its long tumble of natural red hair.

Where others at the table were tense, her features

were relaxed and her approach to the game was casual, good humored, almost disinterested. When the dice came around to her, she placed the few chips that remained in her hand on the line, gave the cubes a smiling toss, made a six and promptly sevened out.

Ballard was right at her elbow and, as she turned with a shrug of indifference, she looked up at him and said, "Lucky no one else believed I was going to win either. They would have lost their money."

She held her hand to her mouth suddenly and her eyes had the look of a little girl who knows she's been naughty and is only amused.

"Gosh," she said. "I shouldn't talk like that. About the money. It was just a slip."

Ballard leaped in quickly. "Why shouldn't you talk like that? You're among friends. And we all know."

"Yes, it's silly," she said. "But you never can tell — there might be spies."

"No spies," said Ballard, a little indignantly, "just members."

"I'm a resident member," she came back. "Jane Carling's the name."

As she said this, there was a sly watchfulness in her eyes, but its meaning escaped him.

"I don't reside," he said. "But I'm Member Three-thirty-seven and my name is Charlie Gillman."

She laughed, a sound of wildness and abandon. "Well, Three-thirty-seven, I'm out of chips. The gallant thing would be to buy me a drink."

"Gallantry is not dead," he said. "Choose your bar."

She gestured to the right side of the room and he followed her down an aisle between tables, noting that she had most shapely legs in dark stockings and was flaunting that extended high mould of waving posterior so exciting to a "fanny man." And he was that, all right, though not exclusively.

He began to lead her toward a bar stool, but she said, "Let's try a booth. It's much more comfortable."

"As long as we park," he said.

"That's what I always used to say to my dates," she returned with a chuckle. "As long as we park."

The remark, from such a pretty girl, carried overtones of excitement, though as he sat down he wasn't sure he had understood. He played the words back. Yes, she had said them.

When they were seated a waiter approached, took their order and returned almost immediately with the drinks.

"How do you like the Topsiders Club?" she said, sipping her Whisky Sour, taking the cigarette he offered and tapping it on a beautifully manicured nail of pale pink.

"I haven't had time to decide," he said. "I'm still an observer."

"Oh, you'll like it," she said. "It's different. The whole idea is so clever, too."

"I had it explained to me," he said, "but I still don't quite understand how the payoff works."

"Didn't they send someone around to talk to you about it?"

"Oh, yes. But at the time I was tied up with some important work and I'm afraid my mind wasn't on it."

"Well," she said a little impatiently, "it's so simple, really. The prizes, of course, are a dodge. I mean, they really do give the prizes — no doubt about that. But it's only so the members will appear to have some reason to play games that would be silly unless there was some incentive. And also it acts as a cover for the bookkeeping end of it. Every chip you take is charged against you.

And every one you bring back is credited. Then, at the end of the month, if you're a loser, a bill comes to you in the mail. It will be for all kinds of phony club services, even including banquets that you never heard of. But you'll know that you're paying for your losses when you mail the check. Gambling bills will have a tiny gold star in the top center."

"Suppose you lose so much money that even a big service tab would be ridiculous?"

"Then you are reminded in a little form notice that you have pledged, say the sum of forty thousand six hundred dollars to the club charity fund."

"And what happens when you win?"

"Once a month an envelope containing the cash will be delivered to you."

"Oh, sure, I remember. But one thing I don't think anyone mentioned was what happens if you decide after a bad month that you don't want to pay?"

She gave a little sardonic laugh. "Don't be silly, dear. They'd send around one or two of their boys and the whole thing would get very unfriendly. Shall we talk of something else?"

"For instance?"

"What interests you."

"At the moment you do."

"And at the moment, Charlie Gillman, I am also interested in you. You're a very sexy hunk of man."

She punctuated this with a long, careful look and a smile that he could feel creeping all over him. He didn't know what to make of her. She was such a lovely bundle of female, intelligent, poised. But strangely uninhibited.

"And you're a very sexy hunk of woman," he said.

"Now we're on my favorite subject," she said. "I adore sex."

"I beg your pardon?"

"I said that I simply adore sex."

"My God," he said, "shall we drink to that?"

She held up her glass and he touched it with his own. "To sex," she said.

They drank.

"You're terribly frank," he said. "There should be more women like you — I suppose."

"Women are a terrible bunch of hypocrites," she answered. "Don't you think? I mean, they're always pretending that sex is one thing that just never, never enters their sweet little minds and that the whole subject is degrading, unless, of course, there are all kinds of rings and papers. I would think that men would get so bored with that junk. Heavens! You must see right through it."

"Oh, we do, we do!" said Ballard hastily. "Drives me nuts, all that coy stuff."

"I got over that long ago," she said with a teasing smile, leaning toward him so that her breasts were more visible than ever beneath the black material.

"How did you get over it?" he said, feeling about the same astonishment he would if he bard gone to church and found a rock 'n' roll combo had replaced the organ.

"It wasn't too difficult," she answered. "I discovered at an early age that I was oversexed. That made it easy. And now I just admit it honestly." She giggled. "And you know," she said confidentially, "when you tell a man that, he stops looking bored. You should see your face right now."

"You're having a lot of fun with me, aren't you?" he said.

"Of course I'm having fun with you. But all the same, I'm telling the truth."

He knew the type. Now and then you met an odd-ball who liked to shock and run. He once knew a girl who would suggest something obscene to a strange man sitting next to her at a bar. Then, when his mouth fell open, she would climb from her stool with great dignity, as though she had never uttered a sound.

"Well," he said, "it makes for fascinating conversation. But I know women. If I made a pass, you'd run fast enough."

"Yes, I would," she said. "I'd run toward you. After all, I'm a resident member."

"So? What does that mean?"

"It means that I have my own snug, cozy little apartment right downstairs. Just one little floor down."

Now, he thought, I'll fix her good.

"Well," he said, "as long as it's only one little floor down, why don't we go get snug and cozy?"

"Mi. Gillman!" she exploded. "Mr. Charles Gillman! Now you're beginning to talk my language. Shall we go?"

"I'll be goddamned!" he said, standing and dropping a five on the table. "Come on!"

Chapter Thirteen

She had made him a drink and he had finished it and now he was looking around at the bright modern living room with its expensive furnishings and he was still puzzled. It was a unique experience and really he was more interested in satisfying his curiosity than his passion — most of which was upstairs with Paula.

"You were right," he said. "It sure is snug and cozy. And dark." She had turned out all but one lamp.

She put down her drink and cuddled close to him on the sofa. Her lips brushed his mouth, his cheek, found his ear and pressed. "Shall I put on something more comfortable?" she whispered.

"Fine," he said. "By all means."

He was going to see how far this would go.

"Do you like to watch a woman undress?" she murmured.

"It depends on the woman. I've seen some on the beach that should *never* take their clothes off."

"You know very well that I mean me. Would you like to see me undress?"

He swallowed, "I wouldn't miss it," he said. "When does it happen?"

"Now," she sand. And with that, got up and slowly, as in a strip tease, removed everything but stockings and shoes.

She had a stunning figure and he had expected to be very excited. But actually, he was unprepared. Jane Carling's approach to sex was too sudden, too blatant.

She sat down next to him and he felt a little disgusted.

"You look as though you still haven't figured me out," she said.

He nodded. "It's true."

She went away and came back wearing a negligee.

"Didn't they tell you about the resident members?" she asked.

"No."

"They're mostly girls, you know. But there are a few male members. But the whole thing was designed for us girls. You understand?"

"Finally," he said. "Yes, finally."

For the first time she looked at him a little suspiciously. "Are you sure you're a member?" she said. "You don't seem to know anything at all about what's going on."

"You want to see my card?"

"No, but . . ."

"You see, Jane, it's this way. I knew about the setup, but I didn't realize that you — I mean, you looked so . . ."

"I gave the cue — resident member. That's all I'm supposed to say, that I'm a resident member. And you're supposed to know what that means."

"I see," he said. "It means that you're willing and available — but not free."

"Exactly."

"It's supposed to be a hundred, isn't it?" he guessed.

"A hundred for short little chats like this. Two hundred if all-night sleeping arrangements are involved."

"Haw many girls ate there?"

"About sixty right now," she said.

"I saw some very pretty girls tip there and, I was wondering, but not sixty."

"They only allow ten on the floor at a time," she said. "Otherwise it would be obvious. It works in shifts. About every hour a new group gets a chance."

"So if I see a pretty girl, all I have to do is go up and say hello and ask her if she's a resident member?"

"Sure. You can tell by the attitude, anyway. You won't get a snub."

"Very neat," he said. It was. Just about foolproof. You were talking to a fellow member and you went with her to her apartment and whose business was that? Of course, if there was an exchange of money . . .

"Naturally, I'll be billed in some disguise or other," he said.

"Naturally."

"Nothing so vulgar as an exchange of cash."

"Much too vulgar," she said.

"And risky," he said.

"True," she said.

"Does the management provide the apartment free?"

"Quite," she said smiling. "And the food. And forty percent of the take."

"Marvelous," he said. "But they must be feeding the police department something, too."

"I wouldn't know," she said coldly. "But without money passed, they'd never prove anything. Anyway, you didn't come down here to talk business, did you, sweetie?"

"No. And as a matter of fact," he said standing, "I don't have time for play, either. I'm supposed to meet someone upstairs — a non-resident member."

"Better stay," she said. "They watch, you know. And you're checked in, so it will cost you. Besides, I kind of like you, sweetie — and it would be a pleasure."

"Maybe some other time," he said. "Meantime, just charge it, honey. Just charge it."

He went out.

Not ten minutes later, as he was watching the play at the roulette table, Paula came by and gave him a tight little nod. Immediately he left and went down to the lobby. He arrived almost as soon as they began to page Mr. Charles Gillman.

Paula sounded breathless. "I have news," she said. "I think it's what you want."

"Good deal, sweetheart. You're a fast worker."

"I would have been faster, but I couldn't find you."

"I was checking on the cleverest and the biggest call-girl operation I've ever seen."

"What!"

"Never mind. I'll explain later. Call girl is a very loose term. What's up?"

"I was looking at the picture of the *Sea Jet* and telling Russ how much I liked it and that I wished he'd take me for a cruise. And he said maybe in a few days, that right now it's at the boat yard having some work done on it. I assume by boat yard he means East Coast Marine in Lauderdale. Thought you might want to check it tomorrow."

"Not tomorrow, Paula. Tonight."

"Tonight!"

"Yes. If there's a chance it's at East Coast, every second counts."

"Oh, dear. You will be careful, darling. You will be extra careful. I couldn't stand it if . . ."

"I'll be careful. Just worry about yourself. How goes with Smiley?"

"Still smiling and still chasing — but not catching."

"Well, keep your track shoes handy until I can get through to our boy. I've got a big, fat message for him. Listen, you're not going to stay in that house tonight with Gould around, are you?"

"No. I'll go back to my own apartment. Call me there. It's in the book."

"Will do. God knows when. Some time before dawn. Meantime, think you can handle him?"

"You just don't know men. Some of the worst are the easiest — for a woman. They're all children."

"I'll remember that — you've given yourself away. 'Night, sweetheart. Have to hit the trail."

"'Night, darling. Lots of luck — and love, too."

"Ditto on both. Until later."

He hung up.

Chapter Fourteen

*E*ast Coast Marine in Fort Lauderdale, some twenty miles north of the outskirts of Miami, was located west of town on New River. After checking the address in the directory, Ballard had no trouble finding it as he knew the area like no other.

East Coast was a large boat yard under an immense, open-ended shed with dockage space running several hundred feet along the river. A variety of yachts and boats of many sizes were tied up at intervals along the sea wall of East Coast's property. Under the shed could be seen the dark outlines of yachts and small craft set on platforms for viewing. On the street side there was a large glass-enclosed office and display room from which came a dim light. This, Ballard guessed, would contain, besides boats and equipment, sales offices and a desk or two for the detail work of the business.

On the water side of the office there was a towering fence and wire-mesh gate. At this hour, 1:40 A.M. by

Ballard's watch, the gate was closed and padlocked. To enter and locate the *Sea Jet,* Ballard would have to pass through the gate or through the door to the office. Since both were locked, the chances weren't good. Further, there was an armed uniformed guard. Ballard could just make him out, seated far in the back of the office, reading a magazine. Probably the guard would make the rounds once every half-hour or so.

Ballard waited. Just before 2 a.m., the guard stretched, yawned and departed. He returned in about ten minutes to resume his place. Ballard could figure now on something like a half-hour leeway, providing he could get inside.

Obviously he wasn't going to be able to break in. So, after a careful inspection of the fence, Ballard followed it to where it terminated at the river. Here he lowered himself over the sea wall. It was necessary to submerge his feet in the water, but by inching along hand-over-hand, he made it to the other side of the fence and hoisted himself up silently. After removing his shoes, he drained them of water and tied them to his belt by the laces, one on each hip.

He moved forward soundlessly on stockinged feet, peering closely at names on sterns of yachts tied up along the river.

These craft were the largest to be seen and he wasn't going to look elsewhere because he did not believe for a moment that the *Sea Jet* had been hauled to a dry dock. *Swift Guild, Aqua flight, Jessie 11, Barracuda . . . Sea Jet!*

The *Sea Jet* took up the space at the farthest extreme of the dock from the office and the guard. Good! Ballard had recognized the yacht and the name was only a confirmation. The gangway was in place, but the yacht appeared to be dark.

Ballard put on his soggy shoes and climbed softly

aboard clutching Beef Costigan's .32 revolver. He saw no shadow of a guard. He listened, could hear nothing. He sneaked around the familiar deck to the after-cabin. He slid back the door and stepped in, closing it. Pausing at the companionway, he peered below.

There was a soft, nearly invisible spill of light from under a door forward on the port, the water side. He crept down the companionway, tiptoed over the deck to the door. He listened. There was the sound of a man's voice, held low but clear. The voice had a surly, menacing quality. It droned on, paused, continued, but went unanswered. Ballard knew the voice. It belonged to Needle Nose Tabrino.

"You play along with me," Tabrino was saying, "and I'll go easy with you. You don't fight me and I'll let you up a while. Either way, I'm gonna get it from you, bitch! And I got till morning."

Ballard crouched and looked into the keyhole. There was a single dim light. A porthole had been covered with a heavy blanket. Below this there was a bunk. And tied to the bunk was Maxine Bowman. A gag was tightly wedged in her mouth. She wore a tan sweater and green skirt. The sweater had been pulled up to her neck, a torn brassiere dangled, exposing her great breasts. Needle Nose sat on the edge of the bunk and ran his hands over her flesh.

"You gonna play nice?" he said.

She shook her head and immediately he began to wrench up her skirt.

Ballard tried the handle of the door cautiously. It was locked. He stood back from the door and knocked softly but firmly.

"Who's 'at!" Sharp, nervous.

"It's The Ox," he said, dropping his voice and making it guttural. "Open up, Tabrino."

There was a flurry of movement, a metallic sound. A key turned, the door opened warily. The barrel of a submachine gun nosed ahead of Tabrino.

Ballard dropped the .32 in his pocket, pushed safely inside the barrel and grabbed it, ramming stock into belly. At the same time he gave Needle Nose a swift kick on the shin and the gun came away in his hands.

He was stepping in, reversing the weapon, when Needle Nose, recovering quickly from small pain and large surprise, booted him in the crotch and followed with a body blow to the chest that had the power of desperation.

Ballard groaned, clutching his groin; the gun clattered to the deck. Believing Ballard to be temporarily helpless, Tabrino stooped for the weapon and caught a kick in the shoulder which sent him sprawling. He danced to his feet, backed, groped behind him and came up with a sawed-off baseball bat in his hand. Raising it, he moved in.

Ballard turned and caught a glancing blow on his left forearm. The arm went numb and the anger came upon him with a rush. His right fist detonated against Tabrino's jaw. He swayed off-balance, dropping the bat and taking a left to the mouth that had small effect since Ballard's bruised arm was still partially numb.

Tabrino's fists were coming up to protect his sharp features when Ballard delivered such a heavy right to his pointed beak that he was in real danger of having to change his name. And now the lower part of Needle Nose's face was a crimson wash. He began to fall when Ballard's fist crashed teeth into his mouth, sank unconscious when Ballard splintered his jaw.

Ballard stood over him a moment, watching. "That's two down, you filthy bastard," he muttered. Then he untied Maxine, removed the gag.

Tears were in her eyes as she sobbed, "Gill! My God, Gil! How did you ever . . ."

"Never mind," he said. "Later. No time."

As she stood, adjusting her clothing, rubbing her wrists; Ballard took the ropes and bound Tabrino, placed the same gag in his bleeding mouth. Then he plucked the gun from the deck, found it fully loaded and cocked, said, "Come on!"

They moved quietly down the gangway. Ballard now remembered that the fight had been quite loud. If the guard had left the office, the sounds might have been audible . . .

The Thompson gun was familiar to him. He had fired one like it a time or two on a police range. Now he held it ready and guided Maxine in the darkness. It was going well. The light burned as before in the office and midway to the gate there was no sign of the guard.

But now, as they approached a high platform where a speedboat was enthroned, a brilliant cone of light washed them in its glare, falling suddenly from some high point above them to the right. They froze with surprise, then rushed on as a bullet whined off the cement at their heels and the explosion echoed from behind the light.

Ballard shoved Maxine to the protection of boat and platform, kneeling beside her. The cone followed, splashing around their hiding place.

They were trapped.

Ballard lay prone and bellied his way to tire edge of the platform, cradling the gun in his arms. He was sweating with fear, clammy under his armpits. In his life he had known much tension and much deep worry, though seldom more than the nudge of fear. It was the first time he was so frightened he had to command his scattering thoughts to make his body obey. Any action was dangerous. But inaction was fatal.

He poked the gun around the corner of the platform without showing his head. Instantly a bullet splintered wood just above him and instantly he gave eye to the sights and fired a short burst well above the light. He did not want to kill the guard. It was scare-firing. The ugly rattle of the gun would force the guard down, and the torch with him.

Ballard heard quick movement, but when the light held, he knew it was fixed. Perhaps a searchlight mounted on the bow of a boat. His mind was functioning again and he moved swiftly. Chancing exposure, he sucked in his breath, aimed and fired directly into the beam, stock pulsing against his shoulder, the *pock-pock* of the Thompson an evil reverberation under the shed. The light winked out with a thin splatter of glass.

Listening, he detected the movement of someone climbing from a perch. The guard, if he was that, apparently had not been hit.

Now Ballard nudged Maxine and they ran toward the office. No time for the slow fumbling around the fence by the sea wall. Another shot followed their movements but was wild in a darkness broken only by the dull glimmer of yellow through the glass of the office door.

Ballard fired high overhead in the direction of the shot and they reached the door, plunged inside. He felt, rather than saw, movement behind. Hard metal pressed his back.

"Drop it. Quick!"

Ballard could not drop the gun. Now or later it would cost him his life and probably Maxine's. He knew this in an instinctive flash. Holding the gun rigid, he whirled with the speed of movement for which he had once been famous in pigskin battle, lifting the barrel high. It caught the man across the side of the head and he collapsed without pulling the trigger of the .38 Police Special, falling sideways unconscious.

In amazement, Ballard was looking down at the uniformed guard. Then, who. . . ?

He found out soon enough. There were feet scuffing cement, approaching from the shed. Ballard pointed to a desk and motioned Maxine down behind it. He spied the guard's torch, grabbed it, flicked the light switch. In the darkness he dropped behind a desk parallel to Maxine's and waited.

The steps grew louder, stopped. A great shadow paused in the doorway. Ballard sighted the Thompson around the desk and with his left hand pressed the flash button. Ox Kowalski was framed massively in the doorway. In the glare, his bandaged and bruised face was grotesque, lopsided from the beating Ballard had given him. He was squinting into the light, bringing up a rife.

Ballard fired a staccato burst a good yard to the right of his head. "The next one will cut you in two, Ox," he shouted over the echo.

The Ox flung the rifle to the ground as though it were a snake and raised his hands.

"Kick it here," said Ballard.

The Ox gave it a forward shove with his Foot, keeping his hands high. Ballard picked it up and, at that instant, there was the wail of approaching sirens.

It was not a time for conversation with the police. There would be questions for which he did not yet have answers — especially for the uniformed cops of Broward County. He gave the rifle to Maxine and began to back off with the Thompson trained on The Ox, who had heard the sirens and looked confused.

"Face the other way, Ox," be said. "Get on your belly, hands forward."

The Ox obeyed.

"Not a move," said Ballard. "I'll take care of you later."

He went with Maxine to the glass-paneled door. It was locked. The sirens were growing in volume and number. No time to hunt a key. He kicked the glass in with his foot cad they stepped through the jagged hole. They ran to the car.

Ballard tossed the weapons on the back seat and they gunned away.

He was watching in the rearview. The Ox came bounding from the doorway. He ran, circling a corner of the building. In seconds a car came around the same cornea and hurled itself after him. He knew it was The Ox.

Even as The Ox burned rubber in back of Ballard, a trio of squad cars screamed, red-flashing, out of a side street. Two flounced to a stop before the building, the third gave chase behind The Ox.

"God damn!" said Ballard. "More trouble. The Ox after us and a prowl car right on his tail."

"Oh, God, God!" said Maxine, trembling beside him.

Ballard swung too fast around a curve and nearly overturned. Righting himself, swerving back, he lost ground and The Ox gained. In the mirror there was an orange flare, and a bullet slammed the rear deck.

"Should have known he'd have a hand gun, too," said Ballard. "No time to search him. Max, can you fire that rifle?"

"I think so." Weakly.

"You just aim and pull the trigger. Grab it from *the* back seat. Forget the Thompson."

Maxine got the rifle.

"If he shoots again, aim low. Try to wing a tire. You won't, but it will keep him busy."

"Look!" said Maxine. "The police car is gaining on him and . . . and they're shooting, too!"

Ballard took his eyes from the hurtling road long enough to see the red dome-light not fifty yards behind The Ox, flame jets spurting from windows, while the siren was bleating against the night.

Meanwhile he plowed through empty streets, horned through intersections and prayed.

"The Ox is slowing!" said Maxine.

Ballard glanced at the mirror. The prowl car was pulling abreast of The Ox, forcing him off the road. Both cars came to a halt and man-shadows leaped out.

"The Ox has had it," said Ballard, smiling and wheeling left on the federal highway. "He pulled the cops right off us. First decent thing he ever did in his life."

"Oh, my God," sighed Maxine. "Oh, Christ in heaven, what a night! Hurry somewhere and stop. I'm going to be sick."

"Better sick than dead," said Ballard. And settled to a safe and comfortable pace.

Chapter Fifteen

*M*axine parted the curtain slightly and looked out a side window of Ballard's apartment to the street.

"Think anyone would look for us here?" she said nervously. "I mean the syndicate boys."

"Hell, no," said Ballard, leaning against the little bar.

"With The Ox in jail and Needle Nose tied and gagged, who's to tell Gould he should be looking? Unless when the guard comes out of it he . . ."

"No," said Maxine, moving away from the window and gulping a finger of bourbon from a glass she held with a hand that still wouldn't stop trembling, "the guard was playing at straight. He didn't know anything."

"I had a hunch he was straight," said Ballard. "For that reason alone I didn't want him to get shot. But where did The Ox come from?"

"Ross had him sleeping in one of those boats under

the shed, in case of trouble. I'm surprised he didn't hear you the first time, when you were looking for the yacht.''

Ballard smiled. ''Just luck. I got my feet wet and that gave me an idea. I took my shoes off.''

Maxine sank onto the sofa, took another slug from her glass, sighed. ''God Almighty,'' she said, ''the trouble you went to. And the risk! For me. Why?''

''Beneath my placid exterior,'' said Ballard, ''I have the Rover-boy instinct. High adventure and all that stuff.'' This was true and he knew it. But only part of the truth.

Maxine shook her head. ''I can't swallow that. There must be more.''

''There is,'' he said. ''And I may tell you. Right now, I'll ask all the questions. Don't you think I rate some answers?''

Maxine looked at him steadily. ''Gil,'' she said reverently, ''right now I don't think there's an answer in the world I wouldn't give you.''

''Thanks,'' said Ballard. ''First, how did they get you?''

''Want the full story, all the gory details?''

Ballard looked at his watch. ''It's going on three-thirty,'' he said. ''And there are a lot of things that need doing before this mess cracks open and people begin to run. There's no time for details.''

''I'll make like a telegram,'' said Maxine. ''I was in bed. Right after you left, Needle Nose and The Ox rang the bell. I thought you had come back for something. Like a dope, I went to the door. They told me to get dressed, Russ wanted to see me. I did. But afterwards I was scared and wouldn't leave and I got slapped around. Tabrino gave me a bloody nose.''

''What about that needle in the toy panda's nose? Did you put it there on purpose?''

She nodded. "I thought you might look for me and catch on."

"Smart," he said. "I got the drift right away. So then?"

"So then they took me away. It wasn't really light yet and there was no one around. The sea was like a pond and they had a skiff with an outboard. First they rowed and then they started the motor. The *Sea Jet* was anchored about a quarter mile off shore. Russ was on board. He had been watching the apartment house with high-powered binoculars. First thing he said was, 'Who was the beef-trust brought you home?'

"I was amazed he didn't recognize you. Must have been the distance. But to play it safe, I said you were just a guy in show business I met at the Tropic Owl. He slapped me around but I convinced him. Then they pulled anchor and went to a house owned by one of the syndicate wheels. It was on a canal and . . .'"

"The house where they held the meeting?" he said.

"How did you know? Were you the one who —"

"Yes," he said. "Paula told me about the house and I — went looking for you."

"That saved my life," she said.

"Why?" Ballard plucked ice from a bucket on the bar, dropped it in his glass, added bourbon.

"Because Russ was ready to kill me. I kept pleading with him but his face was like a round smooth stone. He said he had orders to get rid of me, that I knew one thing too many. Oh, the bastard, the cold-blooded bastard. But then you came along and kicked up all that fuss and they didn't know who it was. Maybe a cop looking for me. That made Russ jumpy. He decided to hold me until he could run it down. He has ears all over the police departments. If someone suspected, he would change plans, fly me to another state in their private plane and arrange a little accident. So they moved the yacht to East Coast Marine where they could keep it under guard.''

Ballard began to pace the room. "Who were those men in the meeting and what was it all about?''

"Don't ask me for names. But they're the little big-shots who are going to operate a multi-million-dollar gambling and prostitution racket in Dade County, and then when the fix is in, Broward County, too. That's what the meeting was about. Needle Nose told me that and a lot of other things when he thought I'd had it and it wouldn't make any difference if he bragged a bit.''

"You say gambling and prostitution. You mean in clubs like the Topsiders?''

"My God! You know that, too? How?''

"Later. What about it, Max?''

"Yes, clubs like the Topsiders. A whole lot of them, mostly with space leased from hotels. It's supposed to appear innocent so that if an honest cop took a look, he wouldn't see much. And if he suspected, he wouldn't be able to prove anything. Besides, he'd meet all kinds of resistance at the top. The Syndicate shoved in new politicians and the politicians reshuffled the police force and carne up with a fixed deck. Russ thought up the whole scheme and Chicago sent him to operate it. It's going to be the biggest racket that ever hit Florida.''

"Maybe," said Ballard. "What was in those boxes they took off the yacht?''

"Gambling equipment and crooked gimmicks. With small to medium bettors, they'll play the averages, heavy bettors they'll take, but good.''

"It figures," Ballard said. "I've got the big picture. The details can wait. Let's get to the important part. Gould, alias Salvatore Giuliano, is a killer in a nice clean white shirt, wearing a nice clean white smile. And if he ever gets the chance, he'll kill you, Max. And you know it. So now are you willing to spill what you know to the police?''

She studied him, frowning. "I still don't understand what you're all about, Gil. But yes, I'd tell. And what good would it do? He's got the police snowed all the way to the top.''

"Bull!" he said. "There's no such thing as bribing the entire police force of an entire county. There are always honest cops — close to the top, too. And I happen to know at least a couple. And they know an honest DA. So, how about it? It's your only hope, Max. Otherwise, you're a dead duck sooner or later.''

She was thoughtful. "All right," she said. "I'll give you enough to blow Ross and the Syndicate to hell and back. But first, you answer this: who is Gil Ballard and what is he really all about? And don't tell me you're just one of the boys. Because I no longer believe it.''

"Fair enough," he said. "I'm just Gil Ballard, ordinary citizen with a hell of a big chip on my shoulder. And I'll tell you how it got there.''

He did.

"And this makes you an ordinary citizen?" she said afterward. "You're either a complete nut or Superman with all but the wings. Either way, I like you, Gil Ballard. You're much man.''

"Thanks for the roses, pal," he said. "But I ordered lilies, for Russ, dear, undeparted Russ. Start growing, honey. Let's talk about murder.''

Maxine shuddered visibly, fired a new cigarette from the stub of an old one. "It's too late to talk about murder," she said. "Much too late." She chewed her nails. "I feel so guilty that I didn't . . .''

"Never mind. It's understandable. You were scared senseless. What did you hear that time you were listening, Max?''

"I — well, I heard them talking about getting rid of a man by the name of Paul Vulpiani. And his wife Anne, because she knew . . ."

"God Almighty! The ones who disappeared?"

"Yes. Paul Vulpiani used to be connected with Russ and the Syndicate in Chicago, though I never knew him. He was a builder and an architect. I don't know much about his background because they talked mostly of the plan to get rid of him. But I gathered that he put up a den or two around Chicago for the Syndicate, and Russ brought him down here to design these club layouts. He had the plans for the whole setup. Then he got religion."

"Religion?"

"Don't ask me what religion. I just heard that he joined some sect and decided to reform. Reform and inform. There was a Judge Hoffsteader and he —"

"William J. Hoffsteader, who also disappeared?"

She winced. "Yes, that one. He was a member of the same sect. And when Vulpiani decided to reform, he turned the plans, complete with names of operators and fixed officials, over to the judge. And the judge was going to act on the information, call a special session of the grand jury or something. But the same night of the afternoon he got the evidence, he and his wife were kidnapped and murdered by Russ, The Ox, and Needle Nose. They were taken away by boat just as I was, only they were dumped into the sea."

"Jesus!" said Ballard. "I suppose they were properly weighted down."

"I suppose," said Maxine wearily.

"How did they know Vulpiani had talked?"

"He wasn't a very good actor and they suspected him. So they had a Syndicate man he wouldn't recognize follow him. And when he met with the judge in some hotel lobby and turned over the plans, the Syndicate man was sitting right behind them, listening.''

"Why didn't they kill Vulpiani immediately?''

"Because they had to watch and see if he had any other contacts, if he had told anyone else. He hadn't — except Anne Vulpiani. And when the judge disappeared, he was too frightened to make a move. He knew they were on to him. He was getting ready to sneak out of town when they caught up with him and his wife. They were taken away by car to the yacht and dumped into the sea like the other two. You want to hear the details? I got them all from Needle Nose.''

"I'll listen when you tell it to a police lieutenant I know. Time is important now. Of course, you'll be a witness, but have you any concrete evidence?''

She shook her head. "Not very much. Just this.'' She took off her shoe and stocking, removed something from the toe. She held it up. It was a diamond ring. "This belonged to Anne Vulpiani,'' she said. "Her initials are inside the band with an inscription from her husband.''

"Where did you find it?'' said Ballard, coming over to inspect it.

"*Sea Jet*,'' she said. "Floor of the same cabin where they held me.''

"Hold onto this,'' said Ballard, giving it back. "It may be more important evidence than your testimony. Now, about the gambling clubs and prostitution racket — is there any way this can be proved?''

"Yes. There are plans. There are figures, names of operators and records. They talked about it right in front of me when I was on the yacht because they didn't think it mattered what I knew then. Russ has all that stuff in a hidden safe at his house.''

"A lot of good that does us unless the police get a warrant and by that time I'll bet the safe will be empty.''

She smiled. "In his more trusting days, Russ

opened that safe lots of times in front of me. He used to mumble the numbers and I have a good memory. But you'd have to deal with Carl, the chauffeur. He's usually around."

"What about Gould?"

"I heard Needle Nose say he was going to stay at The Oasis this first night to see that everything ran smoothly."

"Tell you what, Max. You show me that safe and help me get it open. I'll handle Carl, somehow. Then I'll turn you over to a police lieutenant who'll give you protection until Russ and his boys are behind bars. Okay?"

Maxine looked dubious. "And then I'll be out of it?"

"I promise. Except for your testimony."

"Then I'll do it. And God help me if Russ —"

"He won't," said Ballard. "Let's go!"

Chapter Sixteen

W on't be long now," said Ballard. "Couple of minutes more."

They were passing the Hollywood Hotel on their
left. A few smaller splashes of light and it grew dark
along the deserted coast highway.

"I wish I hadn't agreed to this," said Maxine beside
him. "I've got the shakes all over again." Pitifully, she
was scrunched down in a corner as if to hide. She hadn't
said a word for miles.

"Try not to worry, Max. The worst is behind. Besides, we're armed like a tank: Thompson gun, rifle,
thirty-two revolver."

"You going to take all that into the house with you?"
said Maxine nervously.

"No. I'm going to leave the rifle and the Thompson
locked in the trunk. That kind of artillery just gets in
the way when you want to move fast. I never could
understand what Tabrino was doing with a submachine

gun.''

"It gives him a special sense of power," said Maxine. "He's crazy. Worse than The Ox."

"What part do those boys play in this setup?" asked Ballard, adjusting the rearview for the third time and still seeing nothing.

"Strong arms," said Maxine. "Russ's Gestapo. They do all the dirty work and they have their little troops under them, like Carl. They were once mixed up with the Anastasia mob. So was Russ."

"Murder, Incorporated?"

"Yes. A nice career. Specialists."

"What about Beef Costigan? Where does he come in?"

"He's just a drop for messages, a communications center for Russ, a petty crook out of Chicago. Russ is never seen with boys like The Ox and Needle Nose. But once in a great while he meets them at the Gold Reef."

"Like the night I happened along at the wrong time?"

"Maybe it was the right time," she said.

"What would make a guy like Gould, a smooth operator, take a chance on working over a perfect stranger like me because I played some record once too often?"

"A personality quirk," she said. "Russ is an egomaniac. He can't stand to have anyone cross him openly. I've known him to be magnanimous about some sneaky deals pulled on him, big deals, cleverly smoked. He can respect a really smart operator who outmaneuvers him. He works that way himself. But I've seen him mad enough to kill somebody who openly flaunted him over some silly thing. Once he beat a man half to death who stole a parking space he was waiting for. I told him that quirk was going to get him into deep trouble some day.

And you see, I was right."

"So he's big stuff, but down underneath he has a petty streak," said Ballard.

"He's full of contradictions," she said. "Passions, frustrations, fighting intelligence. He's positively weird when you get to know him."

"Here we are," said Ballard, braking. "House looks dark."

"Don't let that fool you," said Maxine, sitting up abruptly. "What are you going to do now?"

"If we go sneaking around, someone's going to get shot. Best way not to have any shooting is the direct approach." He turned into the drive. "We'll go right up and ring the bell. Such honest behavior will startle old Carl right out of action."

"My God, Gill" Maxine whispered. "What if Russ is home?"

"You said he wasn't. But if he is, he won't catch on until it's too late. He'll avoid trouble on home grounds unless he thinks it's Giuliano's last stand."

Maxine was only able to moan as Ballard parked at the door and doused the lights. "Squat down and stay right where you are," he said. "Until I call you. Leave the motor running, doors locked. If there's big trouble, drive off fast and get the police. Okay?"

"Be careful," whispered Maxine. "Please!"

Ballard got out and rang the bell. He waited and rang it again. After an age, a light came to life behind the door. There was the sound of a latch sprung and Carl stood in the doorway. He was wearing sneakers over bare feet, slacks and the jacket of his uniform half-buttoned, revealing a swath of coarse black hair winding up his chest. He had the look of alertness pushing against sleep.

"Morning, Carl. Russ home?"

Carl was squinting, not yet able to make out Ballard in the exterior gloom. At the mention of Gould's name, his hand came out of his jacket pocket — empty.

"Not here," he said. "Who're you?"

Ballard stepped forward into the light. The .32 came easily into his hand. "There," he said. "If you can't recognize me now, don't bother. Just check the gun. Thirty-two caliber, fully loaded."

"Whatta you want, bastard?"

Carl had recognized him. He moved back slightly.

"You know my name, Carl?"

"I heard it. Ballard. But it don't mean nothin' to me. Whatta you want?"

"Just a peek at some papers in the safe, Carl, old buddy — Maxine!" he called over his shoulder. "Come on! It's okay."

He heard the car door opening and, in a moment, she stood by his side, creating untold surprise in the eyes of Carl.

"Aren't you. going to be polite and invite us in?" said Ballard.

Carl backed away and they stepped in, locking the door behind them.

"Search him, Max. No, not that way, Max. From behind, out of range. That's it."

Maxine produced a small automatic from Carl's jacket, found his trousers empty. Ballard dropped the weapon into his pocket.

"Max," he said, "you know this house. Any rope around?"

"In the kitchen," she said, "there used to be some clothesline. Shall I look?"

"Please. And don't dawdle."

Maxine was back in seconds with a long loop of new line. "Where would be a good place to take him, Max?"

"Upstairs," she said. "In his own room where no-body would stumble onto him." Her voice had gained confidence.

Ballard shoved him ahead up the stairs, Carl taking them to his own small room at the end of a hall. There, while Maxine held the gun, Ballard tied him neatly and improvised a gag out of one of Carl's handkerchiefs he found in a bureau. Even if the push-button door was locked, it could be opened from the inside, so they merely closed it and left him. Ballard followed Maxine downstairs into the den. She gave it light, closed the door, pulled the drapes.

"Now what?" said Ballard.

Maxine hauled the rug back, but Ballard could see nothing but a parquet floor. Maxine walked across the room to an open-mouthed, toothy mounted barracuda. She stuck a finger in the mouth, felt around, pressed. A floor panel slid back, exposing the round door and dial of a heavy safe.

"Great!" said Ballard. "Now go to work."

Maxine dialed, tried the door. It wouldn't open.

"Must have made the wrong turns," she said and tried again, this time with success. She pulled the door up and back.

Ballard got on his knees, placing the .32 on the floor beside the safe. He reached in. First came a large stack of banded currency. "Cigarette money," he said, laying it on the floor. Then came some long rolled sheets of paper. They proved to be labeled sketches of buildings and floor plans. Beneath these were two large loose-leaf notebooks and a small ledger. He examined them.

The ledger contained building cost estimates, fig-ures on furnishings and gambling equipment with ex-planatory notes. One of the loose-leaf notebooks bore typewritten pages detailing the operation of the clubs.

The other gave the club names, locations and a listing of personnel in order of importance. Some of the latter was written in ink.

"You recognize this handwriting?" said Ballard.

Maxine looked carefully. "Russ's," she said.

"Sure?"

"Positive."

"Look here!" said Ballard, turning a page. "Names of police officials on the payroll — and their take. My God!"

For a good ten minutes they studied the books and papers. Then Ballard looked up suddenly, cocking his head. "You hear something, Max?" he said.

She listened. "No. Nothing."

"Guess I'm on edge," he said. "Well, apparently it's all here. Gambling setup, figures on the prostitution take and how it operates, names on the payroll, the works. But there's a lot of it and this is hardly the place to make a real study. We'll leave the cash, of course, and take the books to The Man.

He began to put away the currency when there was a small stealthy sound. He reached for the gun as he turned.

"Don't try it, sonny boy!"

Carl stood in the open doorway, clutching a great fistful of .45 automatic.

Ballard slid his hand from the gun.

Carl advanced into the room. Behind him, weaponless but smiling, came Ross Gould. And at his elbow — Paula!

Chapter Seventeen

*P*aula Schaeffer was not looking at Ballard, but at Gould. She was wearing just the trace of a sly smile. There was treachery in the smile. He saw it there and was more amazed than at the sight of Carl with gun or Gould with his sleek, casual expression of dominance.

"Well, well," said Gould, sitting on a corner of a massive desk across the room, folding manicured hands in lap. "What a pleasant surprise, Max. Imagine finding you here. And with the boyfriend, too."

He was dressed in a beautifully tailored suit of midnight blue, white-on-white shirt, conservative gray tie, white handkerchief neatly squared in his breast pocket. There was the suggestion of lithe muscle under the blue jacket. Beneath the dark groom of hair, his handsome olive face was placid, his smile a flashing punctuation to his words.

Maxine opened a red mouth in a pale face and found nothing to say. Her lower lip trembled.

After kicking the door shut with a backward thrust, Carl remained in a fixed position behind a steady gun. Paula stood next to him by the desk, still smiling slightly and always looking at Gould.

"Shove the thirty-two this way, Ballard," ordered Carl.

Ballard obeyed and Carl picked it up, stuck it into his hip pocket. "Now the automatic you took from me, bastard. And don't try to outguess me, lover-boy. If the gun don't come out of your pocket barrel-first, you can shoot it through a hole in your head."

Ballard thought of a quick shot snapped from inside the pocket. It would be a nice dramatic B-movie touch — and just as silly. He brought the gun out barrel-first and slid it across the floor to Carl, who placed it in his jacket.

"I was worried about you, Max," Gould continued, as if this byplay was no more than an annoying interruption. "The Ox got into a little trouble, you understand. Nothing very serious. Still, they locked him up because the police are idiots and they fall into temporary states of confusion. They forget which side they're on. But The Ox was allowed the usual call — to our attorney, you understand. And this attorney made a trip to the station. And while he was there, he had a chat with The Ox. And then with the police. It's all a misapprehension and The Ox will be out in a few hours. Meantime, he told the attorney that you had become . . . lost, shall we say? And naturally when I heard, I was concerned. But I never expected to find you here. No, never. What a truly marvelous piece of luck."

The silence was solid as granite, though Ballard could swear he heard Maxine trembling.

"I don't suppose," said Gould, "that in your present emotional state, either of you could remember what happened to Tabrino during all that ugly disturbance. No? Well, never mind. Max will have at least a reasonable time to discuss it with me later."

Ballard was watching Paula. She still remained next to Carl, leaning on the edge of the desk farthest from Gould, who occasionally gave her a quick side glance. Her face had a curious look of alertness and excitement. There was the cruel shadow of a cat smile hovering perpetually at the corners of her mouth. Ballard was gazing at her directly and knew that she knew it. Yet, she would not give him so much as a darting glance. Instead, she picked up a bronze nude from the desk, a tall piece of feminine statuary with upraised arms. She studied this, tracing the delicate molding with the same long, tapered fingers which scant hours ago had caressed him. Ballard's shock held an irrevocable taste of bitterness.

"Well," said Gould, shifting his position on the desk, crossing his legs neatly and pulling at the crease in his trousers, "let's see if we can make some sense out of what we have here. Your name is Ballard, right?"

"That's right," said Ballard flatly, keeping his face bland.

Gould nodded sagely. His calm seemed so inviolate, his approach so like that of a man coming to common-sense conclusions in the operation of a business, that Ballard had difficulty remembering that there was more here than a dream threat of danger.

"Ballard," mused Gould. "Of course the name had no significance for me and I heard it only from Carl. At the time, I was too busy to make much of it. Then I see this same Ballard in company with Maxine at her apartment and I begin to wonder. Tonight Paula, tells me a man by the name of Ballard has been snooping around playing big shot and asking questions. And finally, by a strange coincidence, I happen to get a call from Beef Costigan who tells me this Ballard is the same wise guy who was taught a lesson in the Gold Reef Bar a few weeks ago. Only the lesson didn't take and the guy is around again looking for real trouble, the kind from which you don't recover." His smile flashed like a signal. "So then I phone Carl and I don't get an answer, though he has a special phone with a private number right in his room. Nothing disturbs me more than employees who don't answer the phone. So I hop right over and what do I find? Carl all trussed up, and Ballard, whom I now recognize clearly enough, robbing my safe, valuable papers and cash strewn all over the floor, Maxine, my dear good friend, giving him a hand."

Again the smile was a punctuation. "And, of course, I realize now I was a little impetuous that night in the bar."

"It was the biggest little mistake you ever made, Salvatore," said Ballard with more courage then he felt.

"True," said Gould magnanimously. "And from our mistakes we finally learn. We learn to act with deliberation arid never in anger. So I want you to know, Ballard, that I respect your industry and your cleverness and that whatever becomes of you now will not be done in anger but with perfectly cool deliberation."

"Thanks, Giuliano, you spick bastard. With all pour fake polish, you're still a petty hood, brave behind musclemen, guns and bankrolls paying off crooked cops. I can read your horoscope five-by-five. Your future is already newspaper history. Someday, you'll be sitting in a barber chair, a Caesar getting a haircut. And two guys with names out of an Italian opera will come in wearing masks and black gloves. And they'll walk up behind you and one of them will say, 'Here's a message for you, Giuliano.' Or, 'The Big Boss wants to see you upstairs, pal.' Something like that. And then they'll blow the back of your head off. And the barber shop will be closed for the day while they cleanup the mess. And a whole chain like you will follow and they'll all go the same way, more or less. That's your future, Giuliano.''

"There," said Gould, with the widest of bright smiles. "You see? I let you finish that whole speech and you never once aroused my anger. I'm learning, don't you think, Ballard?''

Ballard was silent.

Gould scratched his nose with a forefinger, turned to Carl. "You know, Carl," he said, "you've been a bad boy. You should have investigated this one and brought me a full report. That was a bad mistake and I think you should pay up for it.''

Carl shifted in place.

"So we're going to let you handle the whole show here. Now this is the, way it works: we'll remove ourselves from the scene, taking Max with us. Her turn will come later but she doesn't fit into this picture at all. After we are well gone, this is how it should appear to the police: the bell rang and you went sleepily down to the door. Ballard was there with a gun. He forced you in here to open the safe. You knew the combination. Ballard was after the money, obviously. But whatever he was after, the papers will be gone. They'll go with us. At this time of the morning, someone at the door is a pretty suspicious thing. So you had a registered pistol in your pocket which you didn't get a chance to use. Not at that time. And Ballard neglected to search you. But while Ballard was busy at the, safe, you saw your chance and you shot him — unfortunately, in the head.

"That's your story when you call the police, after forgetfully picking up Costigan's thirty-two, which is beyond tracing. As of this moment you never heard the name Ballard. You don't know him from Adam. Got it?''

"Now listen, Russ," said Carl nervously, "I'm not gonna take the rap for this."

"You'll do what you're told," said Could. "This baby is on to the whole thing and we can't have him around. But don't worry, it's a setup. There won't be any fuss. And if there is, you know, I'll spring you out of it. I take care of my own. But remember this, Carl boy. The hand that feeds you can also wring your neck. So don't ever think of allowing yourself to become talkative. Even in jails we could get to you, you know. Understand?"

"Yeah, Russ. Sure. I'll handle it."

Gould's eyes slid to Paula. "What do you think of it, honey? He comes in to steal, he's bound to get shot. Perfectly legitimate, isn't it?"

"Perfectly, darling," said Paula, looking up from the statue she was still fingering. "It has the nice clear ring of justice with just the right touch of irony." She smiled. "If you know what I mean."

"I'm with you," said Could, beaming. "But what's more important, you're with me."

"All the way," she said. "I could have told you that long ago, if you'd only asked me. But why do we wait? Remember, we've got things to do." For just a second, her eyes touched Ballard coldly and slid back to Gould.

"Max," said Could, "gather up those papers and books and bring them to me. All of them."

Maxine gave Ballard a pitying look, swept up the papers and notebooks, brought them to Gould, who was now standing, looking at his watch.

"Give us fifteen minutes, Carl," he said. "And during those fifteen minutes just remember one thing: this guy has nothing to lose and he's liable to try anything. If he moves a hair two minutes from now, give it to him. Then do your waiting before you call."

The sonofabitch is reading my mind, thought Ballard, and his guts sickened. "Don't worry," said Carl. "He ain't gonna be alive if he moves his little finger."

Gould began to gather up the papers and books from the desk. And, at that moment, while his attention was diverted, and as Ballard watched, Paula's hand holding the bronze statue came up swiftly and descended mightily over Carl's head.

There was a meaty thump and Carl sank with a small groan.

Ballard was on his feet before the chauffeur crumpled to the floor. Gould had looked up sharply, taking in the situation at a glance. Paula was bending for the gun.

But Gould was fast. He aimed a kick at the side of her head and she collapsed. He saw Ballard and ducked. The fist glanced off his ear. He picked up a wicked, daggerlike letter opener from the desk and advanced in a crouch.

"That won't help you, Salvatore," said Ballard. "You had your chance. Just keep coming. And smile for me, Salvatore. I wanna see teeth, Salvatore."

But Gould wasn't smiling. His eyes were pinpoints of intensity. Weaving, he drew closer and suddenly the blade rose swiftly, ready to impale Ballard.

Ballard had not been watching the knife so much as the eyes. And when they told him something, he was already on the move, his big football-launching foot coming up and catching the forearm in flight, delaying it, numbing it long enough so that he could step in, grab the arm and twist until the blade fell to the floor.

He kicked it off, said, "Now let's try it my way, Salvatore."

Gould didn't wait to be asked, stabbed two quick lefts to Ballard's jaw and mouth, rocking him, drawing blood. But Ballard, in one of the few livid rages of his life, was insensate. Anger was the opiate for his pain and he caught another blow to the left eye without feeling more than a jar.

His face wild, spittle at the corners of his mouth, Gould was bringing his foot up for the disabling kick to Ballard's groin. That was when Ballard stepped aside and delivered the first real blow of the fight, against the olive thrust of jaw. It sent Gould reeling back to the desk, reaching for a brass bookend which he brought down on Ballard's skull.

Ballard felt a gray dizziness overcoming him. He was on the brink of falling into a dark abyss. For a moment he stood stunned and in that moment Gould smiled, wet lips pulling hock from glistening teeth, a smile remembered in another time, in another approach of darkness.

It was a spur that awakened Ballard's conscious will and, as Gould was bringing up the bookend for the crash that would splinter bone into brain, his smile fell apart, shattered, as teeth, like polished china fragments, spilled back into his mouth.

The bookend fell from his hand and the second and third blows made a crimson squash of his nose and an ugly tear under his eye. He sagged against the desk now and it was too long after his head began to call before Ballard was able to stop the brutal reflex of punishment to that face. He kept holding the body up with one hand and smashing with the other.

Then Ballard was empty and the thing went out of him and he looked up at Paula, a stain of dried blood on her check. She stood with the .45 pressed against Gould's head. And there was such a strange malevolent look of hypnotic intensity on her face that he had to say, "No, Paula. No! Put down the gun. It's all over."

Paula's eyes widened and she looked at him as one coming from a trance and the gun hand dropped to her side.

Ballard let go of Gould and he slithered down. Then he bent over Carl, inspecting him, taking his pulse. "Alive," he said, "but far under. He won't be around for hours and I'll almost guarantee a fractured skull."

"I really didn't care if I killed him," said Paula in a hoarse whisper. "I had to be sure."

Ballard smiled for the first time as he stood with the guns from Carl's pockets. "I'm glad I'm on your team, sweetheart," he said. "I never was sure. That performance should win the bronze Oscar." He picked up the fallen statue and placed it lovingly on the desk. Then, for the first time, he saw Maxine.

She had the wicked letter opener clutched tightly in her hand and she stood in the center of the. room looking at them through the glimmer of tears.

"Never mind, Max," he said wearily. "What ends well, you know . . ."

She broke into dry sobs.

"I know, Max," he said. "The best thing is to keep busy. Tell you what, go see if you can find that clothesline. No use taking chances, even when they look dead."

She stumbled out of the room and came back in a minute with the line. Ballard tied both men silently and with more efficiency than was needed, while the two women sank into chairs. Then he fumbled for a scrap of paper in his wallet, picked up the phone on the desk and dialed. For some time he listened.

"Ballard, Lieutenant. You said if it was important, if I had it in writing, if people would talk, you . . . I know it's goddamned near five o'clock in the goddamned morning! But I've got Maxine Bowman here ready to talk like a boarding-house landlady, I've got reams of papers and records on the whole syndicate operation with names on the payroll, including also a few of your buddies on the force, evidence of four homicides as you call them, and . . . Where am I? You know how to get to Salvatore Giuliano's place in Golden Beach. . . ? Twenty minutes? Sure, I've got company. I could wait longer. No one here's going anyplace. See you, Kohler. So long.''

He hung up.

"Max," he said, "do me a favor. One of the last. Just sit there and hold this gun. Not that they'll get up. But I worry. And I don't feel so good. And I need air. Okay?"

Max nodded and took the gun.

"Come on, Paula," he said.

They sat outside on the patio and the tropic morning was an innocuous whisper, denying violence.

"How did you ever convince him," said Ballard, "that he could show his fine Italian hand in front of you?"

"I had to take a lot of pawing," she said. "I had to pretend I didn't care how he got his money. I had to play it like a moll. I had to make him think that if you were his enemy, nothing was too bad for you. And I had to promise to marry him."

He sighed. "Mrs. Salvatore Giuliano, first lady of the Mafia. Well," he said, "this is where we met. Was that only a few days ago?"

"No," she said. "Another century."

They were silent.

"Thanks, Paula," he said. "That's all I've got for now. Later I'll pin medals."

"Stay out of barrooms," she said. "And don't play records."

"Not on jukeboxes," he answered.

They were silent again.

"Paula," he said. "Do you think we'll ever get back

to normal things, like maybe croquet and mah-jongg?''

"Too strenuous," she said. "But give me some sleep and I'll try to get back to normal, darling. I'm willing to try."

Softly, her head on his shoulder, she began to weep.

www.ingramcontent.com/pod-product-compliance
Lightning Source LLC
Chambersburg PA
CBHW022155260626
47155CB00018B/2054